Some gratitude . . .

Fargo pulled the Navajo boy off the Ovaro, scanning the area for any *vaqueros*. When they realized their captive was gone, they'd be out for blood.

The boy climbed the hill dutifully, his chains clattering. Fargo found the going rough, the dirt under his feet crumbling and slippery. Then, without warning, he felt a sharp punch from behind.

He fell forward, twisting as he went. He landed heavily on his side, momentarily shaken by the hard impact. Quick hands snatched his Colt from his holster before he could recover. The click of the six-shooter's hammer being cocked sounded louder than the rumbling thunder. Fargo raised his eyes and looked down the barrel of his own gun, staring at death—to be delivered by the young Navajo he had just risked his life to rescue. . . .

THE
TRAILSMAN
#227

NAVAJO
REVENGE

by

Jon Sharpe

A SIGNET BOOK

SIGNET
Published by New American Library, a division of
Penguin Putnam Inc., 375 Hudson Street,
New York, New York 10014, U.S.A.
Penguin Books Ltd, 27 Wrights Lane,
London W8 5TZ, England
Penguin Books Australia Ltd, Ringwood,
Victoria, Australia
Penguin Books Canada Ltd, 10 Alcorn Avenue,
Toronto, Ontario, Canada M4V 3B2
Penguin Books (N.Z.) Ltd, 182–190 Wairau Road,
Auckland 10, New Zealand

Penguin Books Ltd, Registered Offices:
Harmondsworth, Middlesex, England

First published by Signet, an imprint of New American Library,
a division of Penguin Putnam Inc.

First Printing, September 2000
10 9 8 7 6 5 4 3 2 1

The first chapter of this book originally appeared in
Nebraska Slaying Ground, the two hundred twenty-sixth volume in this series.

 REGISTERED TRADEMARK—MARCA REGISTRADA

Printed in the United States of America

PUBLISHER'S NOTE
This is a work of fiction. Names, characters, places, and incidents either are
the product of the author's imagination or are used fictitiously, and any resem-
blance to actual persons, living or dead, business establishments, events, or
locales is entirely coincidental.

The Trailsman

Beginnings . . . they bend the tree and they mark the man. Skye Fargo was born when he was eighteen. Terror was his midwife, vengeance his first cry. Killing spawned Skye Fargo, ruthless, cold-blooded murder. Out of the acrid smoke of gunpowder still hanging in the air, he rose, cried out a promise never forgotten.

The Trailsman they began to call him all across the West: searcher, scout, hunter, the man who could see where others only looked, his skills for hire but not his soul, the man who lived each day to the fullest, yet trailed each tomorrow. Skye Fargo, the Trailsman, the seeker who could take the wildness of a land and the wanting of a woman and make them his own.

New Mexico Territory, 1860—Fort Fauntleroy,
situated between Dinetah *(Navajoland)*
and the malpais *badlands:*

Slavery, no matter who is the slave, is evil.

1

The cavalry had been after Skye Fargo for three days. The rangy, lake-blue-eyed man known as the Trailsman dismounted from his Ovaro and walked to the edge of the steep-walled red sandstone mesa, and looked down the slope at the blue-clad column struggling along the twisting trail. A bright New Mexico–summer sun burned at his weathered face and caused sweat to run in small rivers from his brow. Fargo wiped it away with his bandanna unconsciously.

He heaved a deep sigh and knew he could not keep running from the U.S. Army for long. They were too determined to find him. Settling on a rock, he let his Ovaro rest while he took in the incredible view of the territory. Two of the Navajos' three holy mountains lay to the west and to the north, rising majestically amid a purplish haze. Far to the east lay Santa Fé, but it was a fool's errand trying to pick it out because of the winding mountains and the *malpais,* the blackened volcanic stone badlands that turned ordinary land into deadly stretches only the best—or most desperate—could cross.

The Trailsman was the best, and even he found the going hard.

He cocked his head to one side and listened to the horses' steel shoes clicking against stone, the rocks dislodging and tumbling a hundred feet down to the desert floor, the creaking of saddle leather, and the swearing of the troopers. Taking a deep breath, Fargo caught the scent of sharp sage with a hint of sweat and lather from the horses. For three days they had pursued him. Fargo had just wanted to enjoy the scenery and relax for a few days, but the army had been persistent. It was definitely time to find what such dedication meant.

The leader of the column struggled over the mesa rim and spotted Fargo immediately. If the Trailsman had wanted to hide, this cavalry captain would have hunted throughout the territory for a hundred years and never found so much as a hair from Fargo's head, but Fargo thought it was time to end the chase, as much for his own peace of mind as for the struggling horse soldiers.

"Howdy, Captain. What can I do for you?" Fargo said.

"Mr. Fargo, you're a hard man to run down. Why were you trying to get away?" The captain dismounted, took off his canvas gloves, and tucked them under his broad black leather belt. The man was older than Fargo had thought from the easy way he rode, perhaps in his early forties. He had a direct gaze and an honest face. This bothered Fargo even more because he knew what the captain was going to ask of him.

"I don't want to scout for the army," Fargo said. "That's what you were going to ask, wasn't it?"

"You read more than trails, sir," the captain said. He thrust out his hand. Fargo shook it, noting how firm the captain's grip was. "I'm William Chapman, commanding officer of Fort Fauntleroy."

"The new fort right at the edge of Dinetah?"

"Yes, sir, that's the one. We're at the periphery of Navajoland and entrusted with keeping the peace."

"The Navajos have been peaceable enough of late," Fargo said. "They might skirmish with the Pueblos, but I haven't heard anything of them raiding settlers."

"That's been changing, and it's not just because we built the fort," Captain Chapman said. He settled down on the rock next to Fargo and enjoyed the same view for a moment. Fargo wondered what Chapman saw.

The Trailsman saw frontier, wild and free and open for a man to make a name for himself or to just pass through. Fargo worried that the captain saw something else. A land to be settled, plowed under, and farmed, fenced off and grazed. A land for cities to sprout up like toadstools after a rain.

"What's changed," Chapman went on, "is the slave raiding. The Mexican settlers are complaining that their women and children are being taken by the Navajos. The white settlers call the Mexicans *los ricos* because they've got established spreads and more money than they can shake a stick at."

"Slavery's going to eat this country up alive," Fargo said. Men—and women and children—had to be free. Not ought to be, *had* to be. That was the way he lived his life and the way he believed everyone ought to.

"The Navajos claim *los ricos* are stealing *their* children and hustling them out of the territory, taking them south into Mexico. And now the white settlers are claiming the Indians and bands of slavers are preying on *their* women and children. It has to stop."

Fargo said nothing. The captain was right. Such inhumanity had to be ended.

Captain Chapman turned and stared earnestly at Fargo. "Sir, I won't mince words. I need your help. I need the best scout I can get to track down whoever's responsible so I can stop the slave trading."

Fargo had not been sure what the captain was going to use as an excuse to recruit him as a scout. He had worked for the army before and many times it had been a tough and dangerous job. Still, people he knew and respected got along all right with the military. Kit Carson, working as an Indian agent over in Taos, had no fight with the army. If anything, he helped whenever he could. Other mountain men of Fargo's passing acquaintance had worked for the army, too. Ceran St. Vrain even boasted of it, but then he would boast about making the sun come up, if anybody would listen to his tall tales.

"Pay's terrible. Food's even worse. Fort Fauntleroy has just gone up and lacks many of the amenities of more established posts."

"So what's in it for me?"

"Satisfaction at doing your duty, Mr. Fargo. That and twenty dollars in danged near worthless scrip a month."

Fargo sighed. "With such generous terms, how can I

refuse?" He thrust out his hand, and the captain shook it.

Fargo looked past the cavalry officer at the vista stretching forever. This was his kind of place, where he could stand and imagine riding anywhere in the world. A young child stolen from his mama and papa and put into slavery would never share this feeling of utter freedom. He had to see to changing that.

Fargo mounted his Ovaro and started to work right away, leading the column down another less steep trail, and headed directly back to Fort Fauntleroy, his new home for a while.

The town just outside Fort Fauntleroy, Ojo del Oso, was pleasant enough. The construction didn't seem much different from any of a dozen other places in New Mexico Territory: mostly adobe, with some attempts to erect stone houses and buildings. The people were friendly and greeted him as he rode through. Fargo saw a few whisper to friends and relatives as he passed. Fame was a bit hard to bear, especially when he had not done anything to deserve it among these fine people.

"You must be the new scout over at the fort," greeted a florid man with muttonchops, all the rage back East, or so Fargo had been told.

"I am."

"Come on into my store," the man said, ushering Fargo inside the adobe building. "Even if you don't buy anything today, it's cooler inside than out. That sun can fry a man's brain."

Fargo stepped into the dim cool of the general store and looked around. He needed some ammunition for his Henry rifle, and maybe a blanket to replace the one he had used for more than a year. It had become threadbare and the merchant had some fine Two Grey Hills Navajo blankets.

"You like 'em?" the man asked. "I traded for those blankets off a soldier who captured them during a raid."

Fargo ran his hand over the fine, distinctively patterned wool blankets, then moved on. If a soldier had "captured" them, he might also have stolen them. Fargo

4

wanted no part of that, since it might incite any Navajo he came across as he tracked slavers to their lair and brought the full might of the U.S. Cavalry down on their heads.

"Reckon all I need today is a box of ammo for my rifle," he said.

"Here, it's on me. I'm Austin Kincaide, fort sutler. I'll put it on the captain's bill." The man smiled broadly, showing a gold tooth in front.

"Papa, aren't you going to introduce me?" came a voice like wind blowing through the tall ponderosa pines. Fargo turned to face the woman in the doorway leading to a back room. He touched the brim of his hat.

"Ma'am," he said, eyeing her. She was a real armful, this filly. Several inches shorter than Fargo, she had eyes as blue as the sky and lustrous blonde hair that fell below her shoulders. Her oval face seemed too fair for anyone living in Ojo del Oso, but Fargo was not complaining. This young woman was a vision of loveliness.

"That there's my younger daughter, Dorothea."

"You have another daughter? If she is half as lovely, you are a man doubly blessed, Mr. Kincaide."

"Aren't you the charmer?" Dorothea said, moving forward, her skirts softly sweeping the floor of the store. She smiled prettily, then eyed him the way he had been eyeing her. Dorothea seemed to like what she saw as much as Fargo did.

"Luella's betrothed," Austin Kincaide said, "but Dorothea is an old maid. The ugly duckling of the family."

"Old maid?" Fargo's eyebrows arched at this. "Ugly duckling?"

"Why, I'm only twenty-two, Papa. That's not so old. Do you think I'm too old to marry, Mr. Fargo?"

"Never too late," Fargo said.

"Luella's got herself pledged to Jack Sawyer. Perhaps you know him," Kincaide said. "He works at the Silver Centavo."

"He's a cardsharp and a cheat," Dorothea said acidly. "Don't make Texas Jack out to be anything more, Papa."

5

"You're just jealous of your sister. Now git on into the back and straighten up, child, like I told you."

"Very well, Papa." Dorothea batted her long eyelashes at Fargo before turning and going. As she vanished into the back room, she looked over her shoulder. The smile she gave him was anything but demure and set Fargo's pulse to pounding.

"Don't pay her no nevermind. She and Luella never got on too good, even being sisters and all. When their ma died, it sort of drove them apart."

"Don't think you have anything to worry over, Mr. Kincaide. Your daughter's likely to find herself a beau. A woman that pretty won't go unmarried for long."

"She's had offers from the officers at the fort," Kincaide said, almost too hurriedly, as if explaining Dorothea's unmarried condition like he might some disease. "But she didn't take to them, though I think she looks favorably enough on the captain."

Fargo heard someone enter the store and wondered at the flash of anger that passed over Kincaid's face. The store owner hurried to the man, a Zuñi from the look of his clothing, and the two spoke in low tones for several seconds. The more Kincaide talked, the madder he got.

"Anything else I can do for you, Mr. Fargo?" he called.

Fargo picked up the box of cartridges for his rifle and tipped his hat in the sutler's direction. Almost immediately Austin Kincaide went back to his whispered argument with the Pueblo Indian. Fargo stepped outside into the hot sun, again aware of how fast a man might die in this country. His tongue felt like it had been wrapped in cotton and he needed a beer to wet his whistle.

Fargo headed for the Silver Centavo Saloon down the street. He was more interested in seeing who Dorothea's sister was marrying than getting a beer, but he had gone only half the distance when Captain Chapman came galloping up, his horse lathered and the officer agitated.

"Mr. Fargo, glad I found you. There's been another raid. Out near the Zuñi pueblo. A half-dozen young

6

boys were stolen away by Broken Finger at a nearby watering hole."

"Who's Broken Finger?"

"A Navajo trying to make a name for himself as a war chief. Manuelito and the other chiefs won't have anything to do with him. He's just trying to prove himself."

"The Zuñi village about fifteen miles from here?" asked Fargo, walking to his horse and swinging into the saddle. He settled down, reached back, and dropped his shells into the saddlebags. It was a good thing he had not had that beer. It might have robbed him of needed senses.

"That way," Chapman said, pointing to the southwest. "We'll be riding fast, so I only brought a dozen men with me."

"I can make better time on my own," Fargo pointed out.

"Mr. Fargo, it would be best if the cavalry handled the matter of the slavers."

Fargo shrugged. He understood what the captain said—and didn't say. The brass over at Fort Union wanted the cavalry to settle the matter to enhance their prestige and power in the area. Fargo found it more tedious riding with the soldiers and worried that the raiding party might slip back into the rugged Canyon de Chelly. Not anyone, other than a Navajo venturing into that red-rock spired canyon, ever returned.

No one.

"Let's see that watering hole," Fargo said.

"What do you make of the tracks?" Chapman asked Fargo.

Skye Fargo stood and walked along the dusty trail. Rock and sand made tracking almost impossible, but now and then a horse stepped into the dirt or made an impression that remained, even after a puff of wind came to erase it.

"Indians," Fargo said. "They are riding in that direction." He pointed due west.

"I'd think Broken Finger would hightail it for the safety of Canyon de Chelly."

"You just might have it backwards, Captain," Fargo said. He took off his floppy big-brimmed hat and waved it through the air so the sweat would evaporate and cool him a mite. For three miles Fargo had followed this trail and could only come to one conclusion.

"What are you saying?" demanded Captain Chapman.

"Looks as if the raiders are Zuñis, not Navajos."

"But you said there were Navajo tracks!"

"There are. If that's Broken Finger, he's chasing after the Zuñis, not running from them," Fargo said. "That's where the Zuñis took four or five young children from a Navajo band of mostly women back at the watering hole, where we found evidence of the fight."

"That's not possible. Everyone knows Broken Finger is the one taking the slaves."

"Not saying he doesn't have a few," Fargo allowed. "What successful Navajo warrior doesn't have a couple of wives and a few slaves? But the slavers this time are the Zuñis."

"Might you be wrong about this?"

"Might be," Fargo said, "but I don't think so." He put on his hat, pulled down the brim to shield his eyes, and looked into the setting sun. A particularly rocky area drew his attention. This was the sort of place where water pooled, bubbling up from underground hot springs. And the kind of place Indians out on the trail stopped to rest.

"Are the slavers ahead?" asked Captain Chapman.

"Let me do some scouting," Fargo said. "If I signal, you come running. Fast."

"All right," Chapman said, not liking the way Fargo liked to do things on his own, but seeing no way to get around it.

Fargo set off at a gait his Ovaro could maintain all day and long into the night, but mostly he wanted time to study the trail and think. Everything seemed turned upside down from what the captain had told him. Fargo slowed and studied trampled grama grass and the dirt under it for a spell.

For the world, it looked as if the Navajos pursued the Zuñis. The Navajos weren't called the Lords of New Mexico for nothing, having superior horses. At times, Fargo marveled at their horsemanship. The Zuñis were less well versed, being farmers tending crops instead of warriors ranging far and wide across the countryside. The horses in the lead group of eight seemed weaker, smaller, less able.

Before he reached the tumble of rocks where he thought the Zuñis might have camped, he dropped to the ground and left his faithful Ovaro tethered to a low-growing mesquite. The pinto contentedly nibbled at the bean pods still hanging on the limbs, deftly avoiding the long spines.

Henry in hand, Fargo hurried forward, reaching the rocks. He had almost an hour before sunset. The Zuñis might have watered their horses and then ridden on, but Fargo did not think so. He was not sure they even knew the Navajos were on their trail. The Zuñis might have decided to camp by the watering hole.

If so, this place could have turned into a bloodbath.

Like a snake slithering through the rocks, Fargo moved forward until he spotted scrubby cottonwoods growing beside the pool of water. A crude rope corral held eight horses, confirming the number Fargo had thought. And to one of the trees he saw three small Navajo boys with ropes around their necks and their hands bound behind their backs.

They sat stoically, eyes ahead and showing no emotion. He knew what they must feel inside. Not one was older than seven or eight years old. Fargo started circling the camp where the Zuñis laughed and joked, sharing a rabbit. Bones from two others had been tossed to one side.

The Zuñis feasted but offered nothing to their captives.

Fargo's finger tightened on the Henry's trigger, but he could not take out all the Indians before they began fighting back. He needed the extra firepower offered by the cavalry if they were to rescue the boys and ensure their safety. Especially if the Navajos hadn't arrived yet.

9

He climbed to the top of a boulder some distance from the Zuñi camp and lifted his rifle, waving it over his head. Dust kicked up in the distance, telling him Captain Chapman was on the way. Fargo returned to the Zuñi camp, just to safeguard the young boys.

Just after he wedged himself into position into the rocks, where he could look down over the camp and take a decent shot at any Zuñi trying to harm the boys, all hell broke loose.

From three sides came whooping, hollering braves. Fargo blinked in surprise when he saw that only three Navajos attacked the eight Zuñis. He lifted his Henry and sighted in on one Zuñi, shooting him before he could drive his knife into the back of a Navajo warrior.

The Navajo twisted around, saw the dead Zuñi fall, then looked into the rocks and spotted Fargo. Their eyes locked, onyx and lake blue, and there was no camaraderie. Though outnumbered, the Navajos fought fiercely against the Zuñis until Chapman and his squad came storming up.

The bullets flew and ricocheted, and took out two more of the Zuñis. The Navajos did not retreat, even when the cavalry charged up. As they fought on, it was the Zuñis who fled.

Chapman ordered some of his men after them, not seeing that the three Navajos, bloodied from the uneven fight, were now sidling around the watering hole toward the captive boys. From his perch, Fargo watched the Navajos use their sharp knifes to slice through the ropes.

The boys were free. Again the leader's eyes locked with Fargo's. Fargo touched the trigger of his Henry, then lifted the barrel and just waited.

No thanks, no signs of gratitude. The Navajo leader—who must have been Broken Finger—slipped into the gathering shadows with his two warriors and the rescued slaves.

Skye Fargo wondered what he had gotten himself in the middle of.

2

"That sure was a bust," Captain Chapman complained, as they rode back to Fort Fauntleroy. "Couldn't make head nor tail out of it, either. Those *were* Zuñis being attacked by Navajos, but—"

"Don't fret over it, Captain," Fargo said. He had been riding in silence, thinking hard about everything he had seen. The sheer arrogance of the attack on the Zuñis left no doubt in his mind that the Navajo warrior had been Broken Finger. The fledgling war chief had brought along only two braves to rescue the boys taken as slaves.

Zuñis as slavers and not the Navajos? That did not square with what the cavalry had been told, and what Chapman had told Fargo had been going on in the territory, but seeing was believing.

"We ran off the Navajos. That much was a success, but they got away with the slaves. Wish we could have freed them. Taking slaves is too much of a tradition to stop overnight, but I swear, I am going to try!" Chapman shook his head in dismay at a wasted foray.

"They'll do all right now," Fargo said. He could not claim much expertise on such things, but it looked to him as if one of the boys was the spitting image of Broken Finger. The chief might have been coming to rescue one of his own sons. Or, considering the way the Navajos worked family relations, that might have been one of Broken Finger's nephews he was personally responsible for raising.

However it was, the slaves were in no danger of being sold south of the border. They had gone home where they belonged.

Fargo saw the lights around Ojo del Oso and turned in that direction while the captain and his squad returned to Fort Fauntleroy about a mile farther down the road. Bidding the officer good night, Fargo rode to the saloon he had been headed for earlier when Chapman dragooned him into the scouting mission to find the boys. Almost a day on the trail had done more than whet Fargo's thirst. He was so parched he could drink a barrel of beer all by himself.

Tying the Ovaro to a hitching post nearby, Fargo brushed off some of the dust he had accumulated during his ride and fight, then went on into the low-ceilinged adobe saloon. Coal oil lamps around the walls on ledges intended for *santos* turned the place cheery and almost bright as day. A half-dozen tables had chairs pulled up around them but only two showed any action with card games.

Fargo bellied up to the plank that served as a bar and eyed the men in the nearest card game. He wondered if one of them was Jack Sawyer, Luella Kincaide's fiancé. There was no way of telling since three of the men had the look of professional gamblers out to do in the other two men at the table. Fargo wanted to take those two suckers aside and point out how quickly they were losing their money, but he didn't. It wasn't any of his business how men found enjoyment.

"Beer," he ordered. The barkeep nodded and drew a mug that was more foam than beer. The nickel Fargo dropped on the wood plank vanished faster than a road-runner pecking at a snake.

"Lemme know when you want another," the bartender said, moving back to talk with a scruffy-looking pair of men. Fargo was good at telling a man's occupation by the cut of his clothes, the way he moved, how he looked around at the world. These two didn't herd sheep or tend cattle. Imagining them in a field weeding and planting was beyond him. Whatever they did, it was not likely to be too legal.

"I see the way you're eyein' them gents," said a man walking up to him and leaning both elbows on the plank.

The bar tipped precariously, and Fargo grabbed his beer to keep it from spilling.

"I'm new in these parts. I just wanted to see who ran things in Ojo del Oso," Fargo replied.

The man snorted in contempt, getting Fargo's attention. There was a bitterness in his manner that belied the man's peaceful facade.

"You lookin' to make some money like them?"

"Depends on what they do," Fargo said.

"Rumor has it they're slavers working for *los ricos,* them rich Meskin ranchers." The man spat and missed the cuspidor. He took no notice. "I hate them, I truly do."

"Slavers?"

"The rich Meskins. All the time lordin' it over us poor folk. We got here after them, and they own most of the land, given them by their fancy kind over in Spain two hundred years ago. What right did he have to give any of this land away, especially to them?"

"About the same as we have settling it when the Navajos and Zuñis were here first," Fargo said.

"That's different. They don't own land. They don't want to. They're always movin' round, 'cept the Pueblo Indians. They're all right, I suppose, but they raid just like the Navajos."

Fargo got the notion this gent didn't much like anyone. He finished his beer and left the Silver Centavo, not sure what to do with himself. He stepped out in the street and enjoyed the cold wind whipping down from the mountains. High desert got mighty cold at night, and it refreshed him after a day in the saddle suffering the summer heat. Fargo knew he had a bunk over at the fort but decided to find a place to spread his bedroll in Ojo del Oso.

He heard grunting and curses in Spanish, followed by a woman's pleading voice. Fargo's Spanish wasn't good enough to follow her rapid speech, but it seemed there was some trouble. He cut down a narrow space between two buildings and came out on another street where an old man struggled to hoist two stacks of grain back into a rickety buggy. A woman, probably his wife from the

13

way she watched over him like a mother hen, offered words of encouragement.

"Can I help?" Fargo asked. He grabbed a sack and heaved it back into the buggy, which sagged under the load.

"Why do you do this?" demanded the man. "You are one of them, one of the whites."

The Mexican was hardly one of *los ricos* the gent at the saloon had complained about. His clothing was clean but old and mended. None of the fancy silver conchas favored by the wealthier Mexicans glinted anywhere on his hat or belt or shirtfront.

"That's true, but you needed help. You need some work done on the axle, too, or it'll break before you go a mile." Fargo studied the situation. The locking nut had come loose. "If you tighten the nut while I lift the buggy, you can be on your way safely in a few minutes."

The woman rattled off in Spanish again. From what Fargo got, she was urging her husband to accept the offer of help.

"Are you like that thief? You want much money for this?"

"What thief?" asked Fargo, setting his feet and gripping the edge of the buggy.

"Austin Kincaide, of course. He robs us! He steals our money and sells us bad things!"

Fargo heaved. The powerful muscles across his shoulders tightened as he lifted the light buggy off the ground. The man hurried over and quickly spun the nut back until the wheel no longer wobbled. Fargo lowered the buggy and stepped back.

"Thank you, señor. You are very kind," the woman said when it was apparent her husband was not going to thank Fargo.

"What's your beef with Mr. Kincaide?" he asked, curious.

"He charges Mexicans more than he does whites for the same things," she said.

"He sells—" began the man, but his wife elbowed him to silence. He glowered, then nodded his head just once in Fargo's way. This was all the thanks he could allow himself to give. With that, the man slapped the reins on the mule's rump and got it moving out of Ojo del Oso.

Fargo stepped back and scratched his chin. The town had more going on just under the surface than first appeared. The whites didn't cotton much to *los ricos,* and the Mexicans didn't much like the whites. At least not the storekeeper Kincaide.

Starting for the general store, Fargo stopped and stared as a woman bustled along, her head down and muttering to herself. She crashed right into him, bounced back, and almost lost her balance. Fargo grabbed her arm to steady her.

"Sorry, ma'am, didn't mean to run into you like that."

"I . . . it was my fault. I am in a hurry. I must find him. Soon, now, oh!" The woman stepped away from Fargo and stared up at him, seeing him clearly for the first time. She had dishwater blonde hair and eyes the color of low-grade turquoise. "You're him! The man I wanted. I mean, Dorothea described you and told me—"

"Whoa, slow down. You're Luella Kincaide? Dorothea's sister?"

"I am. She and I had a discussion and, as always, we disagreed. About all we could come up with was asking a favor of you."

Luella was not a bad-looking woman, but for Fargo's taste, Dorothea had all the beauty in the Kincaide family.

"It's our father and what he's doing."

"I heard," Fargo said, remembering the Mexican farmer and his wife's complaints about the sharp ways the storekeeper dealt with them.

"You know? I mean, Dorothea said nothing got by you, being the Trailsman and all, but how did you know Papa was selling Taos Lightning to the Indians?"

This took Fargo aback. He thought she was going to tell him about cheating the Mexicans.

"You want to tell me what I can do for you—and Dorothea?"

Luella took a deep breath. Fargo could not help noticing the rise and fall of her ample bosom under her crisp white blouse. She was better endowed than her sister, but he did not find her any the more attractive for that.

"Please speak to him about selling the liquor. He gets it in from . . . well, never mind who sells it to Papa. But he should not sell it to the Indians. That is the cause of so much trouble here."

"Greed can do that to a man."

"What's that?" Luella looked at him again, as if he had shaken her out of a dream.

"Greed can make a man ignore the trouble he's causing. I don't know if your pa would stop because I told him to, but maybe if I hinted Captain Chapman would find out, that might jolt him."

"Well, yes, yes it might," she said. The woman looked up, batting her eyelids at him. Fargo remembered Dorothea doing the same thing. With her it had been sexy. With Luella, it seemed calculated and turned him wary.

"Call me Lu," she said. "My sister never said you were so handsome."

"I'll talk to your pa," Fargo said, not wanting to carry this flirtation further. She was pledged to Jack Sawyer, after all.

"I'll come along with you. To show you the way," Lu said hastily.

Together they walked to the general store, Fargo aware of how the woman's hip often bumped into his. Then his attention shifted. Something was wrong at the store. It took him a few seconds to figure out what it was.

"Stay here," he told Lu. Fargo drew his Colt and strode around the back of the adobe store. Crates had been ripped open and the contents strewn about. Kincaide's wagon had been tipped over and his mules were gone. He heard a low moan and hurried to the side of the store. Austin Kincaide had pulled himself around, trying to reach the street in front to get help.

Someone had whaled the tar out of him.

"There a doctor in town?" Fargo asked the man, lifting his head up enough so he could breathe easier.

"I . . . I'm all right. They took her. They took Dorothea!"

"Who? Who's got your daughter and beat you up?"

"The Mexicans. Don't know who. *Los ricos*. Four or

16

five vaqueros. Might have been working for Benavidez. Think I've seen one of them in the store with Benavidez."

"Antonio Benavidez?" Luella stood a few paces away, staring at her father. "Why would he want to steal away Dorothea?" Luella crossed her arms and tapped her foot, as if she waited impatiently for an explanation from her father.

"Fetch the doctor," Fargo ordered the woman. "If there's not one in town, there must be one at the fort."

"Papa, why did Benavidez kidnap Dorothea?" She sounded more insistent than ever.

Fargo knew reasons could wait. Kincaide might be badly hurt. From the way he gasped for breath and shuddered all over, a broken rib was the least of the injuries. A lung might have been punctured, although Fargo noted he didn't blow pink froth from his nose or mouth.

"Wants me to clear out. Wants me to leave so I'll shut down the store. Thinks the fort will close if they can't get supplies from me. Ha!" Kincaide's laugh was a rasp.

"Get the doctor," Fargo said in a steely voice that finally got Luella moving.

"Don't let them hurt her, Mr. Fargo," pleaded Kincaide.

"I'll tell the captain and—"

"No! Not that. If the cavalry goes ridin' up, Benavidez will kill her for certain."

"I'll get her back," Fargo promised. He did what he could to wipe the blood off the man's smaller wounds. The worst of Kincaide's injuries were on the inside. Huge bruises already growing on his chest and belly showed how thoroughly his attackers had worked him over. Fargo stepped back when Luella returned with a smallish man carrying a black bag.

Luella fussed over her pa, not accomplishing a great deal, while the sawbones worked. Fargo backed off, looked at the trail left by the fleeing kidnappers and then fetched his Ovaro. Following them would not be hard, but freeing Dorothea might be if they held her in a hacienda surrounded by armed vaqueros.

3

The trail might as well have been painted with white-wash. Fargo had no trouble following the riders through the winding canyons and out onto a level stretch of land filled with grazing cattle. He rode through the small knots of cattle, some of which opened their sad brown eyes to look at him listlessly. The cattle decided he posed no threat and either went back to chewing the grama grass in front of them or drifted back to sleep. For this Fargo was glad. He did not want a stampede started that would alert those he tracked.

He saw the hacienda almost a mile off, outlined as the sun crept up over mountains to the east and shone the first light of day on the rancho. He had to work fast or everyone in the hacienda would be awake, making rescue impossible.

Fargo took a deep breath and tried to think this through. He had followed the trail quickly because the vaqueros had not bothered trying to hide their tracks. They had boldly returned. Had they also innocently returned? Fargo had only Austin Kincaide's word that his daughter had been kidnapped. From what he had seen and heard of Kincaide, Fargo was not sure he trusted him. The man had been dazed from a beating—and his other daughter had claimed the storekeeper was selling whiskey illegally. How far would Kincaide go to hide his bootlegging?

This might be a dispute between crooks. But as Fargo considered that, he decided it did not matter. If Dorothea had been kidnapped, the reason was less important than getting her away safely. Then Benavidez and Kincaide could fight it out over the Taos Lightning, if that was the root of the trouble.

Fargo reached the side of the huge adobe hacienda and looked around. A couple of small children fed chickens in a coop behind the house. Other than the two boys, Fargo saw no one inclined to bother him. He stood in his stirrups. The Ovaro balked, then settled down as he clambered up onto his saddle, catching a viga sticking out of the adobe and using it to pull himself up.

Flat on his belly, Fargo worked his way to where he could look into the inner courtyard. The house had been built in a hollowed box style favored by the Mexicans and the Spanish before them. The rooms were all connected through the courtyard or from doors cut through the inner walls. He remained still for a spell, figuring where the kitchen was, which rooms were bedrooms and sitting rooms, and finally worked around to the southernmost side of the large square building.

The rooms on this side were used for storage—and where Benavidez was most likely to keep a prisoner.

Fargo stood and carefully walked as quietly as possible to keep from attracting attention. The entire house was up now, the sun a thin bright sliver above the horizon. He reached the storage area, flopped on his belly again, and peered over the edge of the roof. Only two doors were barred. He rolled forward, caught the eaves, and then let himself down easily.

Luck still stood by his shoulder. No one had noticed him. The first door was securely chained with a padlock that required either a key or a lot of hacking and banging with a hatchet or hammer to open. Fargo went to the second locked door, this one secured only by a thick wooden bar dropped into U channels mounted on the wood on either side of the doorway. He tugged the bar free and then put it aside. The door swung outward.

Dorothea cringed as light assaulted her. She put up her hands to protect her eyes and said, "Go to hell. I won't give you anything!"

"Looks like you might already be in hell. I'm here to see you out of it," Fargo said, moving to one side so she could see who spoke.

"Mr. Fargo? Skye!" The lovely woman got her feet under her and lunged forward, her arms encircling his neck. She buried her face in his shoulder. Even through the buckskin jacket he wore, he felt the hot tears of joy she shed.

"No time to stand around caterwauling," he said, pushing her away gently. "You up to getting out of here?"

"Yes!"

He grabbed her hand and pulled her along behind. It sounded good but Fargo had no plan to escape the confines of the hacienda. He had found her and now had to play it by ear. Keeping the inner courtyard wall to his back, Fargo edged around until he came to a door leading through the house and to the outside.

"Skye, no," whispered Dorothea. She pointed out what he had already seen. Four vaqueros sat at a table, eating and listening as a burly man with a pockmarked face spoke rapidly to them. Fargo's Spanish was good enough for him to catch the drift. The big man was Benavidez, and he was telling his cowboys what to do today.

"Nothing to concern us," Fargo said. "Benavidez is saying they should go find some stray beeves a few miles north of here." Fargo weighed what to do next. Subterfuge had its place. This was not it.

Dorothea gasped as he strode boldly across the room, exposing himself to the full vision of any of the men eating breakfast. He kept walking, neither running nor dawdling, and reached the outer door without drawing attention to himself. Fargo motioned to Dorothea to follow his lead. She held her head up high, hiked her skirts and started across the room.

Fargo thought she had made it when she turned and looked at Benavidez. A man knows when someone is staring at him. Benavidez jumped as if someone had stuck him with a needle.

"Come on," Fargo cried, grabbing Dorothea's wrist and yanking her outside. He kicked the door shut, whistled for his Ovaro, then looked around for other horses suitable for Dorothea.

"I can ride bareback," she said, seeing a dappled mare tethered nearby. It had not been saddled yet because a young boy was still currying it.

"Take mine," Fargo said as the Ovaro trotted up. He took three quick steps, got to the top of the hitching post, and launched himself into the air. Turning at the precise moment, he landed squarely on the mare. It protested but he grabbed the reins from the startled boy, wheeled about, and took off after the fleeing Dorothea. Fargo was glad she had not stayed around to see if he successfully stole the horse.

Fargo saw that Dorothea was an able horsewoman, but he was glad he had insisted she ride with the saddle. The mare's gait was uneven and caused him to use his powerful legs to their fullest just to stay on.

"Where, Skye? Where should we go?"

"They'll be after us in a few minutes. Benavidez can't afford to let you get away. That might bring Chapman and the entire 5th Infantry down on his ears." Fargo looked around as they rode down a steep hill toward a rocky arroyo. He led the way into the sandy-bottomed ditch. The two horses left some tracks but finding them in the soft sand would take time, especially now that a little wind was kicking up. More than this, Fargo kept to the rocks along the arroyo. When he reached a spot where they could exit without leaving more tracks, he took it.

"Wait up," he called, reining the mare. Whipping out his Arkansas toothpick, he hacked at some greasewood trees, cutting off two large clumps. Again using his knife, he cut a fifteen-foot length of rope from his lariat and tied the greasewood branches to one end. The other end he tied around the pommel.

"Will this hide our trail?" Dorothea asked.

"Not if they have a good enough tracker," Fargo said, "but it'll do until we can think of something else." He jumped onto the mare, holding the rope with the greasewood branches in one hand and the reins in the other. As they proceeded, the wood trailed behind them, wiping out the horses' prints. He set a brisk pace, wanting

21

to put as much distance between themselves and Benavidez as he could before resting.

They zigzagged up and down sandy ravines, across rocky patches and used the greasewood broom whenever there was a chance they might leave tracks. By midmorning Fargo saw Dorothea was wobbling in the saddle and decided to rest. Even the mare he rode was beginning to stumble. If they ended up on one horse, even one with as much heart as the Ovaro, it would put them at a big disadvantage.

"There," he said, indicating a deep arroyo. The cut bank rose high enough to hide the horses from anyone not riding along the edge. Fargo dismounted and led the grateful mare to a spot where she could nibble at some sparse grass. A few yards above them grew knee-high grass, but he did not want to risk being seen.

"Oh, my," said Dorothea, dismounting. She rubbed her curvy behind and smiled ruefully. "I can ride, but it's been a spell since I did so much so fast."

"You did fine."

She looked at him, her blue eyes locked on his.

"You saved me," she said in a low voice.

"My pleasure," he said.

"It will be, Skye, it will be. I want to thank you properly." She stepped closer. He knew he ought to back away. This wasn't the time or place for what Dorothea had in mind. Then her ruby lips crushed passionately into his, and he forgot all about Benavidez and his vaqueros. Fargo put his arms around Dorothea and found her a taut, seductive package. She moved against him, her firm, young breasts crushing against his strong body.

Her mouth moved a little and her lips parted. His tongue began duelling with hers, slipping and sliding back and forth, playing a game of hide-and-seek that aroused them both.

"Umm, nice, Skye," she said. "Does all of you taste so good?" She slithered down to her knees in front of him and began working at the buttons on his jeans. His manhood leaped out, firm and long and hard. Dorothea lightly kissed him and sent a jolt of pure delight rumbling all the way down into his loins.

Then she sucked him in. Fargo went weak in the knees when the woman began using her tongue on him, licking the sensitive underside, then slowly working back down his shaft. Her fingers stroked him gently, even as she licked and kissed his entire length. Dorothea turned her face up and smiled wickedly.

"You *do* taste good all over." Then she dived back down and began using her mouth for things more exciting than talking. Fargo laced his fingers through her long blonde hair and guided her back and forth in a rhythm that built his already stampeding desires to the breaking point. He finally had to push her away.

"You're too good with that mouth, ma'am," he said. "I need to find somewhere else to see if you're equally good."

"Like here?" Dorothea said, sitting back on her heels, hiking her skirt and wantonly exposing her privates. She did not wear any of the frilly undergarments Fargo had thought he would see. Her blond-rimmed nether lips beckoned to him, a magnet pulling his steely pole.

Dorothea sat down, spread her thighs and then rolled back, bringing up her legs so he could mount her. Fargo dropped to his knees, inched forward, and shivered with expectation when the tip of his shaft sank gently into her moistness. Dorothea rocked a few times, heightening the sensation, then reached between her legs, took him firmly in hand, and tugged.

Fargo dropped forward over her, catching himself on his hands. His hips followed her importuning. He felt the crinkly fleece around her core, and then he buried himself deep inside her. He gasped at the tightness and carnal heat boiling out from her most intimate recess.

Dorothea went wild. She twisted from side to side, rotated her hips, lifted off the ground, and did everything she could to take even more of him into her body.

"Yes, Skye, there, oh, yes, do it now. I can't stand it! You're so big in me. Like a stallion!"

Fargo shoved himself forward and then stopped when their groins ground together in an erotic rhythm. He was fully buried in her softly clutching female sheath. It seemed a crime to draw back, but he did. Slowly. His low gasps were quickly drowned out by Dorothea's cries of joy as he rammed back in. He retreated slowly, inch by inch. But the reentry was hard, fast, burning hot with the friction of his movement.

Over and over Fargo repeated this until he realized he was losing control of his own body. He wasn't pulling out as slowly now. He raced, the carnal heat burning away his self-control. When he shoved back into the willing blonde's portal, she screamed and moaned and thrashed about. Her hips lifted off the ground and she writhed back and forth forcefully, as if she were trying to twist off that plug of his hidden away in her tightest passage.

"More, more, please, no, yes, oh!" Dorothea tossed her head about, her eyes closed and biting her lower lip as passion totally possessed her. She gasped and shuddered when Fargo reached under her, gripping her fleshy buttocks and pulling her body firmly into his. And then he, too, lost all semblance of control. Like a shuttlecock, he bounced to and fro, every movement forceful and filled with wild abandon.

His loins felt as if someone had planted a keg of black powder in them. The friction generated by the willing, wanton woman's tightness set fire to a fuse that burned down fast. When the fire reached the powder, he exploded in huge gouts.

Dorothea gasped and clung to him, her fingers cutting into his back as she tried to sit up. Then she fell back and lifted her buttocks off the ground. This way she was able to stimulate herself even more. She shuddered again.

Sweating and tired, they collapsed into each other's arms and lay staring, his lake blue eyes deeply looking into her own. Then Dorothea broke off and put her head on Fargo's shoulder.

"They say you're a good tracker," she said.

"The best," Fargo contradicted.

"Can't rightly speak about the tracking," Dorothea went on, "but there is one thing where you definitely *are* the best." Her fingers glided down his body and

24

found his flaccid length. Squeezing gently, coaxing life back into it.

But Fargo knew they had to move on. Benavidez would find them eventually, if they stayed on his rancho.

"We've got to get to Fort Fauntleroy," he said. "I want to report your kidnapping to Captain Chapman."

"Right now?" cooed Dorothea. She toyed with his member, then saw that the great Trailsman was right about getting a move-on. "Oh, very well. But we're not going to the fort. Or to Ojo del Oso."

"Where are we going?" he asked.

"Back to the hacienda so you can rescue the rest of them."

"Who?" asked Fargo.

"The slaves. Benavidez is trafficking in slaves. Little boys, hardly knee-high to a grasshopper."

"I'll let Captain Chapman—"

"No!" Dorothea sat up, her eyes flashing and her lips thinning to a tight line. He had thought she was determined before. Fargo had not seen utter dedication until this moment.

"The army can—"

"No!" she repeated forcefully. "By the time those fools get there, Benavidez will have moved the boys south, across the border deep into Mexico. You've got to set them free now, Skye." She pushed down her skirts and stared at him. "If you don't, then I'll have to do it on my own!"

"That's mighty risky," he pointed out. "Benavidez knows we couldn't have gone too far, not yet. He might be waiting for us."

"Then he'll be waiting for us," Dorothea said firmly. The young woman pushed back her now dirty blonde hair. "I will not let him sell young boys into slavery! You can't know how awful it is."

"I know," Fargo said. And he did. "I helped free some of the boys Zuñi slavers had taken."

"Sorry," Dorothea said contritely. "I should have realized you would feel the same way."

"We can't go, not yet," Fargo said, staring up into the

azure, cloud-flecked sky. "They'd shoot us off our horses before we got near."

"When?"

"Sundown," he said. "I've got some jerky we can share. And some water. And—"

"And I think I can figure out what all else," Dorothea said, offering a wicked grin.

Sundown came far too soon.

4

"There's no need for both of us to go in," Fargo said to Dorothea, seeing how the sun was beginning to dip into the west behind a jagged ridge. Dorothea Kincaide frowned. Somehow, even with the sweat and dirt and furrowed frown lines, she still looked beautiful. It might have something to do with how she and Fargo had made love all afternoon long. Or perhaps not. Some women had an inner beauty that radiated out, no matter their appearance.

"I need to tell you all that I know," she said.

"Little boys. Slaves. On Benavidez's hacienda. What else is there to know?"

"They are locked up in a shed outside the hacienda. Out back, near the corrals. I saw four or five of them. I can't be sure how many else," Dorothea said, ticking off the points on her fingers as she talked. "They were shackled, so you will have to break the locks."

"Easier to use a key," Fargo said. "Where would it be kept?" He feared the answer might be on a chain around Benavidez's neck. That meant he had to go through all the vaqueros and then deal with Benavidez himself to get it. As pleasing as it might be breaking the man's neck, it was also incredibly dangerous and the odds would be against him.

"The foreman carries it on his belt. I don't know his name, but he is so arrogant. Why, Benavidez offered me to him if he brought in another dozen slaves for sale in Mexico!" Dorothea stamped her small foot in outrage.

"I can get them out of there," Fargo said confidently. Getting back into the hacienda was easy. Making certain the boys escaped was a horse of another color. "Are they all Indians?"

"I think they are Navajos," Dorothea said, "but I couldn't be sure. I only caught a glimpse of them being marched to the shed when they brought me in. They are evil men, Skye. Utterly evil, to do this to children."

"I noticed," he said dryly. Fargo checked his Colt, then made sure his Henry carried a full fifteen rounds in its tube magazine. He was as ready as he was likely to be.

Dorothea hesitated, then impulsively kissed him. "For good luck," she said. "Make sure you come back for even more."

"That's almost enough to guarantee that I don't go at all," he said, smiling. He swatted her on the rump and said, "You take the mare and get on back to Ojo del Oso."

"All right," she said, still not happy with being diverted from helping to rescue the young children.

"Get going and you can be back not long after sundown. I don't think Benavidez's vaqueros will still be hunting for us. There wasn't a sign of them all day long."

"You hid the trail too well," she said. "That's not all you hid well, either." She reached for his crotch, but he batted her hand away.

"Get on along, now," Fargo told her. He put his hands around her waist and picked her up, She was as light as a feather and he dropped her astride the mare. "Don't stop for anything. Just keep riding and you'll be back before you know it."

"I need to check on Papa, too," Dorothea said. "He wasn't looking too good when I was . . . taken."

Fargo started to say something about Luella, then bit back the words. "See you in town," he said. She waved, gave him a smile, and then put her heels to the mare's flanks. The horse trotted off briskly now, having swapped a heavier Fargo for Dorothea's trim body. He watched as she threaded her way down the arroyo, then climbed the far bank and vanished. Fargo squinted, estimating he had almost an hour of sunlight left, and started for the hacienda.

He got there as the sun dropped behind a tall peak, casting long shadows and giving him a chance to move in without being seen. Like a ghost he flitted from one shadow to another, avoiding the vaqueros as they went about their chores. He edged toward the shed near the corral where Dorothea had seen the young boys.

From inside the adobe building he heard whispers too low to understand, but they were definitely not speaking English. He checked the flimsy door and knew he could break it down fast. A bigger consideration was Dorothea's mention of the boys being shackled. It did none of them any good if he got them free, only to be caught because they could do little more than shuffle along.

Two men suddenly approached, laughing and joking. Fargo pressed himself against the eastern wall, disappearing into gray shadows. The two walked on by, and Fargo identified his target. Swinging at one man's belt was a ring of keys. This had to be the foreman who had been offered Dorothea's favors in return for another dozen slaves. Fargo held down his anger. The two men were easy shots, but he did not take them.

Following, he tried to act as if he belonged on the rancho. There might be a dozen vaqueros watching. Or none.

They made their way to the barn. One opened the large door and paused, seeing Fargo for the first time.

He said something and the foreman turned to face Fargo. Fargo gave them no time to react. He shoved them hard. One slammed into the door, tripped, and fell. The foreman spun around, moving as agilely as a mountain lion. He caught himself and twisted to face Fargo, a knife in his hand.

"So, you did not escape. Have you been hiding out like a coward all this time?" the foreman asked in English.

Fargo swung his Colt, buffaloing the hired hand trying to stand up. The way the man thudded to the floor of the barn, the fight was going to be between Fargo and the foreman and no one else.

"You've been kidnapping children as well as women. Is there any room for you to go after old blind men?"

Fargo taunted. He held his Colt but wasn't going to use it. The report would bring Benavidez's vaqueros on the run. He shoved it back into its holster, giving the foreman a chance to attack.

The man did, lunging with his hunting knife.

Fargo knew the instant the foreman was going to strike and was already moving out of the way. The sharp blade sliced past him. Fargo grabbed the man's brawny wrist and turned it hard. Bones snapped and the knife fell from nerveless fingers.

"Aiee!" The foreman's cry of pain died suddenly when Fargo punched him squarely in the middle of the throat. Gurgles from a broken windpipe hardly carried as the man fell to the floor, clutching his Adam's apple as he choked to death.

Fargo felt nothing but contempt for the man. Slavers deserved to be hanged, and this was far too quick an end. But Fargo picked up the man's knife and drove it squarely into his heart, ending his foul life in a rush. He would have done the same for any wounded, suffering animal, no matter how dangerous.

A quick jerk freed the key ring from the foreman's belt. Fargo checked outside. The twilight had deepened now, and it was almost dark. A few fires popped up around the hacienda but most of Benavidez's men were off herding cattle or over in the bunkhouse. Benavidez himself was probably in his fancy hacienda, enjoying the fruits of his illicit trade.

If Fargo could rob him of even a few dollars, that would be good. Freeing the boys would be even better.

He hurried back to the shed, making sure his Colt rested easy in its holster, then found the key that unlocked the door. He kicked it in and looked around, not expecting a guard but wary nonetheless. All he saw were six boys, none older than six or seven, chained to a ring mounted in the adobe wall.

"Hush," he said, slipping inside. "I'm going to free you all." He began trying key after key until he found the right one. He looked into one boy's eyes and said, "Go home. Don't let them catch you ever again."

The boy said something in Navajo to the others. Fargo

decided the last boy, the biggest of the lot, was the one in charge. He replied to the one Fargo had freed, then the boy lit out running. Fargo worked his way down the shackles, freeing one boy after another. Each in turn rushed from the shed and vanished into the dark.

"They've got you chained up special," Fargo said, seeing the new lock on the last boy's leg irons. He tried four more keys until he reached the right one that freed the boy from the ring in the wall. That left his ankles chained together.

"They're coming," the boy said, his dark eyes going wide. "I do not want to be a slave! Kill me!"

Fargo worked furiously to find the key that would unlocked the boy's leg irons. When he couldn't find the right key, he shoved the ring into his shirt and picked up the boy. For a moment, there was no problem carrying the Navajo. Then the boy started kicking and fighting.

"Stop it!"

Fargo stepped out and saw what the trouble was. A vaquero had found the dead foreman and his unconscious amigo. Fargo leveled his pistol while trying to keep the struggling boy over his left shoulder and fired. The report rang out as loud and clear as any warning bell.

Fargo's bullet caught the man high in the chest. He yelped in pain, then simply sat down, clutching his chest. The others rushed from dinner tables, wondering what the fuss might be.

"Quit fighting me," growled Fargo and the boy obeyed. His long strides carried them to where he had hidden his Ovaro. Fargo dropped the boy and started to work on the leg irons again, only to find there was no time left. A bullet sang through the night, missing him by several feet but spooking his horse.

"Come on!" Fargo threw the boy belly-down over the horse's rump. Then he mounted and kicked the pinto into a gallop. The vaqueros were terrible shots and missed by increasing distances, but Fargo worried they would be astride their horses and after him all too soon. He and Dorothea had escaped that morning because there had been time to conceal the trail. Fargo had no such luxury now.

Already Fargo heard hooves pounding after them. The darkness was a blessing, but Fargo could not properly use this since this was strange country to him—but not to the pursuing vaqueros. He had to pick his way carefully. They galloped after him, oblivious to rabbit holes and getting turned around in the dark.

The last thing he wanted to do was circle and come back on his pursuers unintentionally because he chose the wrong arroyo to ride in.

"You know the country?" he asked the Navajo. The boy struggled around behind him, getting both legs swung to one side, and clinging to the cantle to keep from being thrown off. Fargo received no answer other than a grunt, so he kept riding, hunting for a landmark he recognized, some sign he was riding away from Benavidez's men.

He glanced at the sky and knew there was no help there. The heavy clouds hid any stars he might use for guiding. The dark looming silhouettes of the mountains gave no hint as to what direction he rode, either. His one hope was that a sudden summer rainstorm born in those clouds might fill the arroyos with enough water to cut off any pursuit.

Fargo knew it was time to stop depending on such luck and use some of the skill that had won him a sterling reputation. He kept to the arroyos with their sandy bottoms, but this slowed him, so he got the horse up to the other side. The Indian boy said nothing, and just clung along for the ride. With the shackles on his legs, he wasn't likely to go far if he dismounted.

"Are they any closer?" Fargo asked.

The Navajo nodded. This was about all Fargo could expect from his unwilling trail companion. He saw a hollow on the lee side of a stunted juniper and made for it. Fargo hit the ground and pulled the boy off after him, shoving him into the hollow. He put his finger to his lips, cautioning the boy to remain silent. Then he gentled the horse and drew the Henry from its saddle sheath.

"They're near, I feel it," one vaquero said. "I can smell them!"

"That's your own body odor," said another. "You do not bathe, José. That is why you smell like a cow!" This produced a round of laughter from the other riders. Fargo identified four different voices. He started to lever a round into the Henry's chamber, then hesitated. The sound might alert the vaqueros.

The four men rode past on the far side of the juniper. They gave no indication of even noticing that their quarry was close by. Fargo considered shooting them, then knew he dared not. He could kill these four before they realized what was happening, but others of Benavidez's men had to be out scouring the countryside. The shots would bring them running. Fargo could not fight off all Benavidez's men at once.

Chains rattled and the boy spat in the direction of the vaqueros.

"Why did you not kill them?" he hissed.

"It'd bring others down on our necks," Fargo said softly. "Now hush."

The boy lapsed into sullen silence. He was even less pleased when Fargo hoisted him into the Ovaro again and they rode away from the searchers. Fargo recognized some of the land now, even seeing the broad swept areas where he and Dorothea had dragged bushes behind themselves to cover their trail.

"I can get us back to Ojo del Oso now," he told his unwilling amigo. "Maybe I should take you to Fort Fauntleroy and let the captain deal with you."

A clap of thunder caused the Ovaro to rear. Fargo calmed the horse until a flash of nearby lightning ahead spooked it again. He had to dismount and lead the horse to keep it from rearing.

They reached the hidden spot in the arroyo where he and Dorothea had spent the afternoon so delightfully, but now Fargo was worried that the dry gully might fill with a sudden flood of runoff water from higher in the mountains.

"We can take shelter up there," he said, pointing to the far side of the arroyo. He led the horse across to a deep cut in the bank where they could scramble up. "Get down so the horse can make an easier climb of it," he told the Navajo boy.

The boy dropped to the ground with a clatter of chains and dutifully followed closely. Fargo found the going rough, the dirt under his feet crumbling and slippery. As he dropped to his knees, he felt a sharp push from behind.

Hanging on to the Ovaro's reins for support, he fell forward, twisting as he went. He landed heavily on his left side, momentarily shaken by the hard impact. Quick hands snatched his Colt from his holster. A flash of vivid lightning revealed the boy's determined face. The Navajo held the Colt in both hands and pointed it straight at Fargo.

The click as the six-shooter cocked sounded louder than the distant thunder. Fargo stared down the barrel of his own six-gun, death about to be delivered by the Navajo boy he had rescued.

5

"You got it wrong. I'm saving you," Fargo said, his eyes fixed on the young boy. The Navajo's hands never wavered as he pointed the Colt directly at Fargo.

"I will not be exchanged, one master for another."

"I don't suppose you'd believe me if I said there was a cavalry officer right behind you?" asked Fargo. He looked past the Navajo boy to Captain Chapman, who was quietly moving up. The boy either did not hear the officer's approach or was too intent on killing Fargo to notice.

The boy yelped when Chapman reached around and grabbed the barrel, wrenching it up and away. The Navajo tried to fire, but his finger was bent in the trigger guard and could not pull back. Chapman yanked the gun free and tossed it to Fargo.

"You get yourself into the damnedest situations," the captain said.

"Glad to see the cavalry does arrive in time," Fargo said.

"You can thank Miss Kincaide for that. She almost rode that mare into the ground to reach the fort. She found us out on patrol, not too far from here. From what she said, I reckoned you might need some help."

"Not really," Fargo said, staring at the boy, who seemed to fold in on himself, as if he wanted to vanish entirely. The boy crossed his toothpick arms over his thin chest and he sank cross-legged to the ground sullenly, his eyes averted. Fargo walked over to him, fumbled out the ring of keys he had taken from Benavidez's foreman, and finally found the right key to unlock the shackles. The loud click as the lock came free caused the boy to look up, startled.

"You're free," Chapman said. "You want an escort back to your people?"

Without a word, the boy bolted. Fargo started to grab for him, then let him go. He was free and not likely to fall into Benavidez's trap again. If he made it back to his clan, he was likely to tell the story and warn other young boys and girls. Fargo wondered what his role in that tale would be. Then he shrugged it off. The boy was free. That was all that counted.

"What are you going to do about Benavidez?" asked Fargo.

The captain snorted in disgust. "Not a hell of a lot I can do, if you freed all the slaves he had chained up. I need evidence and you let them all go."

"Watch him real close, then," Fargo said. "Benavidez won't be content to give up such a profitable trade in human flesh." He thought for a moment and then added, "I don't think Benavidez is in it alone. Someone is kidnapping the children for him and he is only a conduit down into Mexico."

"He knows who to sell to for the highest price," Chapman said angrily. "For two cents I'd plug him."

"You know your duty, Captain," Fargo said.

"And you've got a job to do, Fargo. Keep scouting. Find everyone responsible for this. *Los ricos* or whites, Pueblo Indians or Navajos. I don't care. Find out and I'll see that they are tried and convicted."

Fargo liked the captain's passion.

"What part of the country you from, Captain?" he asked.

"Indiana. Marion County, born and raised. I miss the green grass and trees sometimes, but out here I feel like I can do something important."

"Stop the slaving and you will," Fargo said. He had been through hell and only now did it all come crashing in on him. He felt as if he could sleep for a week.

"By damn, you are right, Fargo. So what if we can't make charges stick against Benavidez? I'm going to arrest him to put the fear into the rest of *los ricos*."

"You might get lucky," Fargo said. "There might be some evidence left behind." He remembered how he had dealt with the foreman and the other vaquero and wondered how Benavidez would greet him, even with Chapman and a column of soldiers behind him. Not well, he suspected.

"There's no way of knowing until we try. Are you with me or do you want to head back to Fort Fauntleroy?"

"I'm in," Fargo said, although he was bone tired. He wanted to see this through. He might even be of some help to the captain in finding evidence of Benavidez's slaving ways since he had been there so recently. The shed was certainly a place to begin, but there might be other places where slaves were kept.

Fargo turned cold all over thinking the shed had held only young Navajo boys. Did Benavidez also traffic in young girls? They might be held somewhere else on the hacienda. That thought convinced him of the wisdom of paying yet another visit to the ranchero.

Mounting his Ovaro, Fargo trailed Chapman and the small squad of men riding with him. The captain might have presented a bigger force to Benavidez, but Fargo thought this might be better in the long run. Show *los ricos* that they did not merit an entire company and something might get stirred up.

They rode directly to the hacienda, arriving at the front gate. This was the first time Fargo had entered the rancho as an acknowledged visitor.

"Never been here before," Chapman said, looking around in appreciation of all the wealth. "Benavidez knows how to live."

"He's doing it on the lives of others, especially children," Fargo said.

They rode to the front door and dismounted. The burly Benavidez came out, his pocked face a study in anger. He glared at Fargo, then pointed a pudgy finger in his direction.

"I see you have arrested this thief and murderer!" Benavidez ranted. "I will answer your question, Captain, before you ask it! I *will* testify and I want to see him in front of a firing squad for what he has done."

"What's that crime, señor? Letting your child slaves go free?" Chapman was not cowed by the blustering ranchero. "My men will search your place for evidence that you are engaged in illegal slave trading." The officer motioned to his sergeant, who split the squad up into groups of three to explore the grounds.

"This is an outrage! This . . . this *pendejo* kills my foreman and you accuse *me*!"

Fargo held his tongue. If Benavidez raved long enough, he might give himself away.

"There's a shed out back by the corral. Show it to me, señor," Chapman ordered.

"This is an outrage, I say! You will pay for this impertinence, Captain."

"The shed," Chapman said in a cold tone that did nothing to quell Benavidez's fury. The ranchero stomped around the side of the house, his fancy hand-tooled Mexican boots getting dusty. He stopped a few yards away and pointed.

"There," was all Benavidez said.

Fargo went to the shed and saw that the door had been entirely removed. Inside were the shackles he had taken off the boys. Other than this there was no proof anything he had seen was a fact that would stand up in court.

"Nothing, Captain," Fargo called.

"Leave my hacienda, leave my land right now!" bellowed Benavidez.

"I don't think so, señor," the captain said. "Why are those chains in there? From what I see, that's blood on them."

"I chain wild animals. They sometimes hurt themselves. Then I release them and hunt them." His black look at Fargo was unmistakably a threat.

"Captain," said the sergeant, hurrying up. "We found a fresh grave out back. You want us to dig it up and see what's in it?"

"You desecrate graves now?" roared Benavidez.

"This one brutally murders my foreman, and now you want to disturb his eternal rest? Barbarians!"

"Find any trace of other slaves?" Chapman asked.

The sergeant shook his shaggy head. This was what Fargo had been afraid of. Benavidez had a little time to both hide evidence and bury the foreman. Unless they took the hacienda apart grain by grain and splinter by splinter, there was not much hope of finding anything damning.

Captain Chapman turned slowly, looking around. The vaqueros moved toward them, ringing the soldiers. A fight now would get bloody, and fast. Fargo shifted his weight slightly to reach his Colt, should the need arise.

"I'll testify against him," Fargo said suddenly. "And I can find the boys I let go. They'll testify, too."

"Them?" cried Benavidez. He laughed long and loud. "You would believe Navajo children?"

"You seem to have a good memory about who you chained up, Benavidez," Fargo pointed out. "He knows all about it, Captain. That good enough for you?"

"We're going back to the fort, señor," Chapman said. "And you're coming with us. Now."

"What?" Benavidez's eyes went wide with surprise. "You think to take me from my hacienda? With my valiant vaqueros all around?"

"I'm placing you under arrest for illegal activities including slave trading, Señor Benavidez," Chapman said, as if he had not heard the threat. "Please come with me."

"We will not let the gringos take you, *patrón*!" cried a vaquero, reaching for a pistol thrust into his belt. Fargo never let the man draw the six-shooter. He took two quick steps, judged the distance, and unloaded a haymaker that ended in the vaquero's belly. The air gushed from the man's lungs and he dropped to his knees, gasping for breath.

The soldiers swung around their muskets, getting ready for a fight. If anyone made a mistake now, too many men would die. Fargo moved fast and reached Benavidez's side. He grabbed the ranchero's arm and gripped it tight.

"How many of them do you want to bury alongside that foreman of yours?" Fargo said in a low voice.

"*You* will be the one who dies!"

"Maybe," answered Fargo. "But you'll definitely be among those the undertaker has to bury as well." Fargo slid his Arkansas toothpick from its sheath and pressed the sharp edge into the ranchero's gaudy shirt. The honed blade sliced through the cotton fabric and lightly touched skin beneath.

"Wait!" Benavidez called to his vaqueros. "They mean us no good, but we can work this out."

"We cannot let them take you, *patrón*!"

"Tell the others. Tell Villanueva. Tell all the other rancheros what they do to me. If they want a range war, they will get one!"

"Come on," Chapman said, shoving Benavidez in front of him. "And stop making idle threats."

Fargo was not so sure what Benavidez said was an idle threat. It carried the ring of truth. If he didn't do some powerfully good tracking fast and find the boys he had freed so that they could testify, all of New Mexico Territory might be plunged into war.

6

Fargo sat on the rough rock, staring at the ground and trying to figure out what the trail said. He was one of the best—maybe *the* best—tracker west of the Mississippi, but he could not follow a will-o'-the-wisp. The young boy he had released from Benavidez's captivity had run off, leaving a decent trail for a couple of miles. Then, as the Navajo's good sense returned and the fear the boy must have felt at being kidnapped faded, he became cagier.

The Indian boy was so good at hiding his trail he might as well have vanished off the face of the earth. Fargo found scuff marks on rock that might have been made by moccasins. Or perhaps they were only traces left by a sidewinder wiggling through on its way after a deer mouse. The trail grew increasingly faint until he had to give up. He wished now he had not waited so long to begin the hunt. Losing the boy and his testimony meant Chapman had to release Benavidez soon. Without a real witness willing to testify, there was scant evidence against the ranchero.

Even with the boy and his friends, Fargo was not certain how likely anyone in Ojo del Oso was to convict one of *los ricos*. Benavidez had powerful friends, and money spoke loud and clear. Truth was, Fargo was not sure an Indian could even testify legally, much less one hardly ten summers old.

He stood and slowly paced back and forth, hunting for any trace the boy might have left behind. Fargo finally gave up and admitted defeat. The boy was good, and he was in his own territory. Looking into the distance, Fargo saw the sharp red rocks rising like the entrance to Hell itself.

Canyon de Chelly.

No one but a Navajo went into those twisting, turning rocky canyons and got out alive. Fargo had heard there were several ways in and out, but he had never explored the area to know. He had no reason to nose around there, even now. If he had felt a mite more suicidal he might have ridden into the mouth of that high-walled canyon and asked after the boy.

He doubted any Navajo warrior would have listened. And he did not much blame them. They were accused of being slavers when the Zuñis were stealing their children. Even *los ricos* had a hand in spiriting away the young Navajos.

Fargo shook his head. The Navajos were not lily-pure when it came to taking slaves, though. All he had to do was ask the Utes to the north—or the Zuñis. The give and take of slaves between the tribes was almost legendary. Right now, the Zuñis had Chapman's ear, deluding him into thinking the slave stealing went only one way.

He mounted and rode the patient Ovaro back in the direction of Fort Fauntleroy. Fargo was not happy with what he knew he would find there. It had been two days since Chapman had arrested Benavidez, and the temper of the entire region had changed drastically.

And not for the better.

Fargo neared Fort Fauntleroy and saw right away things were not peaceable. The entire fort was surrounded by a knee-high adobe fence to keep in chickens and other animals. Everywhere he looked, the poultry ran about clucking and squawking to avoid the vaqueros crowding into the parade ground. Fargo hadn't seen this much firepower assembled in one place in a long time.

Each of the men looked riled up enough to start shooting, and that made the soldiers walking their guard paths edgy. The situation was a powder keg ready to explode at the slightest spark.

"Let him go!" demanded one of *los ricos* Fargo had seen in Ojo del Oso. He saw how Captain Chapman stood his ground, but the officer was weakening. In the face of so much trouble brewing, it might be easier to let Benavidez go free.

Fargo knew it was easier, but it wasn't right.

He dismounted and sauntered over to stand near Chapman so he could hear the discussion more clearly.

"Señor Villanueva, he is being held on serious charges."

"Unfounded!" cried the ranchero. Villanueva was a slender man, short and wiry with dancing black eyes and a long, thin mustache. He had Colts thrust into a broad wine red silk cummerbund, puffing out his chest like some bantam rooster. His jacket was of a richly textured brocade, and he glinted in the sunlight every time he moved. Fargo tried counting the beaten silver conchas on the man's sleeve and down the sides of his soft leather pants. Any one of them would be sold for more than he was making in a month of riding scout for the U.S. Army.

Villanueva was obviously a rich and very determined advocate for Benavidez.

"We're rounding up witnesses now," Chapman said, but the words fell upon deaf ears. The vaqueros began making low, throaty noises like growling dogs. Fargo straightened, his hand moving toward the Colt swinging at his hip. If trouble started, there would be a powerful lot of men nursing wounds—or pushing up daisies at the Ojo del Oso cemetery.

"He is a fine man, and you have no proof. We demand you let him go. Now, Captain, or—"

"Or what?" Chapman asked coldly. "I don't take kindly to threats, Señor Villanueva."

"And we do not take kindly to such persecution!"

"Hang Benavidez!" cried a man from the far side of the fort. Fargo craned his neck and saw a couple of men from Ojo del Oso clustered together. "We don't much care if he's out there stealin' Injun kids but he's been stealin' our land!"

"It was never their land," Villanueva said, sneering. "We see now the reason for imprisoning our good friend. You think to steal *our* land!"

A vaquero next to Villanueva nudged him and pointed

at Fargo. This set off a new round of accusations that Fargo did not much cotton to.

"Him," Villanueva said, pointing at Fargo. "He is the one who lies about Benavidez. He is responsible for deceiving you. If he has evidence, let him produce it now. Do it now or let our good friend go free."

"What about it, Fargo?" asked Chapman. "You find the boys?"

"Can't say I did, Captain," he answered. "They hightailed it straight into Canyon de Chelly. One of these days you'll have to scout in there if you want to stop the Navajo raiding—and clear up this predicament over slaving."

"Well?" demanded Villanueva. "Where are the witnesses? No, of course there are no credible witnesses."

"I saw the boys Benavidez had chained up like animals," Fargo said, speaking up. "Are you calling me a liar?"

"Yes!" The cry ripped from a dozen throats at the same time. Fargo found himself facing a wall of vaqueros, all with their hands on their six-shooters, ready for a fight. From the smug look on Villanueva's face, it would happen the instant he gave the word.

"Back off, Fargo," Chapman said. "That's an order." The captain swallowed hard, then turned to the rancheros and their well-armed men. Chapman cleared his throat, swallowed again, then said, "I'm letting Señor Benavidez go."

"No!" went up the cry from the side of the crowd. The men from Ojo del Oso began to surge toward the vaqueros. Soldiers hastened to break up the scuffle. Fargo kept his eyes fixed on Villanueva. If the ranchero so much as twitched, Fargo intended to put a bullet through him.

"Sergeant!" barked Chapman. "Release the prisoner." He took a deep breath and walked over to Villanueva and looked down at the shorter man. "This isn't the end, señor. I will not allow slavers to operate anywhere near where I command U.S. Army soldiers."

Villanueva sneered again and said, "Half your country disagrees. What of Canby's brother-in-law, Silbey? And does not the adjutant at Albuquerque have leanings toward the institution of slavery?"

"Colonel Longstreet's beliefs do not get in the way of his duty," Chapman said tartly. "Even if they did, he is in Albuquerque and *I* am here. There will no more slaving, be it done by Indian or white . . . or by Mexicans."

Villanueva threw back his head and laughed, then hurried to greet Benavidez effusively. The two rancheros were quickly surrounded by others of *los ricos* and made their way out of Fort Fauntleroy. Soon the only ones who remained were the few townspeople who had protested releasing Benavidez. Chapman motioned impatiently to his soldiers, showing he wanted the men released now that the Mexican landowners had left.

"You're a marked man, Fargo," Chapman said. "Villanueva carries a grudge."

"I don't think for a second that Benavidez doesn't, too," Fargo said. "If you want me to move on, I will, but you have trouble brewing here, Captain. You might need all the help you can get."

"I know, I know," Chapman said, distraught. "Benavidez is guilty. You don't have to tell me, either. I feel it deep in my gut. But too many others are guilty, as well. I want an end to *all* slave trading."

"What do you want me to do?"

"In spite of what you've been saying about the Navajos, they are still raiding and taking slaves. A Zuñi village was attacked just after dawn today, and Broken Finger made off with a half-dozen young boys. Find Broken Finger's camp. If I can stop him, I think that might end the Navajo predations." Chapman saw Fargo's expression and added, "I'll have the sergeant post a few soldiers, discreetly of course, to watch Benavidez. Does that suit you?"

Fargo wondered if he ought to mention what he had heard about Austin Kincaide selling firewater to the Indians. He held his peace, not knowing what Luella Kincaide was up to in relaying that bit of information. Besides, that seemed less of a problem than the raiding and slave taking.

"You talked with Miss Kincaide about Benavidez kidnapping her?" Fargo asked, his mind turning to the lovely blonde.

Chapman shook his head sadly. "I spoke at length with her. She can't say Benavidez had anything directly to do with kidnapping her. His vaqueros were the ones who were in on it, and his foreman."

"Who is dead," Fargo said glumly, remembering how he had taken the man's foul life.

"Benavidez could argue he knew nothing about it, and what difference does it make now since the criminal has paid for the crime with his life? No, Fargo, this is complicated. I'm up against a well-liked, rich, and powerful ranchero."

"Do you think Villanueva is involved in the slave trade?"

"They all might be in it together. But still, I have no proof. Go find Broken Finger's camp for me so we can pull that thorn out of our side."

Fargo felt as if he was being run off, but he understood the captain's dilemma. If Fargo stayed near the fort, *los ricos* would become increasingly adamant about killing him. A bullet from ambush, a knife thrust to the belly when he least expected it, any of a dozen ways of dying would come his way. Fargo was not afraid of facing up to the threat, but his death would only ignite an already incendiary situation.

"I'll head out right away. Give me what details you can of the Navajo raid so I can get on the trail."

"You're a good man, Fargo. I wish I had a dozen more like you."

"If you did, you'd be in the middle of a real war by now," Fargo said, smiling.

Chapman laughed and slapped him on the back. The captain walked away, looking more chipper. Fargo wished he shared the man's good humor. He went to tend to his horse, then get back on the trail.

From the ridge Fargo could see a fair amount of New Mexico Territory, or so he thought. The winding road heading toward Santa Fé showed some activity, with dust being kicked up by more than a few slow-moving horses.

Or perhaps it was a wagon train heading for Fort Fauntleroy. Supplies came in sporadically. Fargo considered riding down and seeing what he could beg off the wagonmaster. He had been in the saddle for three days trying to track down Broken Finger. The Navajo had proven as elusive as the young boy Fargo had freed from Benavidez's chains. Every time Fargo thought he was getting close, he grabbed and found himself with a handful of nothing.

He appreciated skill, even when shown by others he had to consider his enemy. Fargo tried to learn how Broken Finger accomplished his disappearing act so he could use it himself later. But for the moment, the task was more irritating than educational.

His belly rumbled a mite from lack of rations. He had ridden far and fast in his so-far futile attempt at catching up with Broken Finger. There had been scant time to hunt, and the vittles he had in his saddlebags were mostly gone now.

Fargo turned his Ovaro's face toward the wagon train and made his way down a winding trail leading to the road. As he rode, a sense of urgency grew in him. The dust from the road he understood. Wagon wheels kicked up a powerful lot of dirt as they rolled along on their steel rims. What he worried about was the swirl of riders approaching from the south, and coming on fast.

Fargo reached the road about the same time the Navajo raiders hit the wagons, whooping and hollering. Arrows filled the air, followed by enough lead to drive even a suicidal man for cover. Drivers and the guards on the wagons bailed out and dove for safety rather than trying to outrace an Indian raiding party.

The Navajos used knives to cut through the tough canvas covering the wagon beds, then grabbed whatever they could from what they found. Fargo was not going to take on an entire band of raiders, but he wanted to get close enough to identify those stealing the army's supplies.

"Git down, mister! They'll lift your hair if you don't!" called out one driver.

"Where's the column that's supposed to be protecting

you?" Fargo shot back. Chapman had said all supplies moving in from Santa Fé were to be guarded by at least a squad of cavalry.

"They got decoyed away, I reckon. Back a mile or two along the road, near the waterin' hole. Now you gonna git down or you gonna be content to die today?"

Two Navajos spotted Fargo and fired in his direction. The range was too great for real accuracy, but the shots had been intended to hold him at bay. He made his decision and jumped to the ground, crouching down near the wagon driver.

"You recognize them?" Fargo asked.

The man stared at him as though he had been in the sun too long. " 'Course I do, old son. Them's Injuns."

"Navajo? Zuñi?"

"What's the difference who steals yer supplies?"

Fargo chanced a quick glance and saw Navajo war paint on one warrior. He had been sent to find Broken Finger, but maybe this band would do for Captain Chapman's purposes. The officer needed to claim a clear-cut victory over the Navajos soon or he might lose his command. Fargo didn't doubt Benavidez and Villanueva were already complaining to the territorial governor about Chapman.

"You itchin' to die?" asked the driver. "Let 'em take what they want. We kin always git more."

"They're leaving," Fargo said. "So am I. Tell Captain Chapman what happened and that I'm on the trail."

"Who are you?"

"Scout from Fort Fauntleroy," he said curtly, mounting. "Skye Fargo's the name."

"The Trailsman? Glory be, and I thought we was sore tried by them savages. Now I know them poor varmints are the ones courtin' big trouble!"

Fargo skirted the looted wagons. Most of the goods had been left, with only the small items on top taken. He doubted his showing up when he did had been responsible for the raiding party's hasty retreat. The Navajos might have thought he was the scout for the column supposedly accompanying the supplies and that a couple dozen angry troopers were on their heels.

For a mile the raiders made no effort to hide their trail. Fargo rode along, not bothering to dismount to study the tracks. He could tell what was happening from astride his Ovaro. But when the Navajos' ponies began to tire, the braves turned cagier. In spite of how they tried to conceal their tracks, Fargo still followed quietly like a wake from a boat.

He overtook them at a small watering hole several miles from the spot where they had ambushed the wagon train. Fargo counted noses fast and figured he faced no fewer than fifteen Navajos. He melted into the shadows, which now grew longer as the sun sank behind the Navajos' sacred mountains in the west. Walking as if he trod on eggshells, Fargo got close enough to the camp to watch the braves divvying up the take.

One warrior stood with his back to Fargo, but it was obvious he was the leader from the way he spoke and distributed the booty. No one moved until he let them.

When the Navajo leader turned, Fargo smiled. He had found Broken Finger. Now all he needed to do was follow the Navajo war chief back to his camp so that Chapman could capture him. Even as the thought crossed his mind, Fargo had to sigh.

All Captain Chapman had to do was capture Broken Finger. It sounded so easy—*too* easy.

Fargo sank lower when the Navajos suddenly gathered their spoils and slung them over their ponies' rumps. The Indians mounted and rode off, never once realizing their every move was being watched.

Quietly returning to his Ovaro, Fargo mounted and followed Broken Finger's band as they meandered up one dry wash and down another arroyo until their destination was obvious.

Broken Finger returned home to Canyon de Chelly, the stronghold no white man had ever entered and left alive.

7

Skye Fargo considered the orders Chapman had given him and the trouble brewing all around Fort Fauntleroy and Ojo del Oso. Capturing Broken Finger was not going to put an end to the ruckus but it might go a ways to relieve it for a spell. There was no doubt in Fargo's mind that the Navajo war chief was increasing his raiding activity. It might have been the chief's way of answering the slave raids by the Zuñis and *los ricos,* or it might simply have been his way of gaining prestige among his clan members. The one time Fargo had faced him and locked eye-to-eye there had been no doubt concerning Broken Finger's blood relationship to the boy he had freed from the Zuñis.

That had been a rescue mission. But Fargo did not doubt the Navajo had taken his fair share of slaves, also. From the Zuñis, from the whites, and from the Mexican settlers in the area. Everyone preyed on everyone else. Captain Chapman wanted it stopped.

So did Fargo.

He heaved a deep sigh and pulled down the brim of his floppy hat to shield his eyes from the bright New Mexico sun. Riding toward the canyon mouth set his heart to racing faster and faster. Canyon de Chelly had earned its reputation because of the steep red stratified rock walls pressing in on either side. A Navajo with a rifle could hold off an entire company of soldiers. A dozen could turn back an army.

Fargo worried more about being spotted than shot as he edged toward one soft sandstone wall to prevent any scout on the rim above from seeing him. If the sentries looked straight down they might see him and signal to others on the canyon floor using mirrors or even a few well-timed shots from a rifle. But riding along one rough stone wall exposed him fully to anyone on the far rim. He realized then this was not a mission of force but of stealth. If the shooting started, Fargo knew he would not be the one ending it.

Canyon de Chelly had a primitive, wild beauty to it, but Fargo wanted a more sedate cemetery for a final resting place. He rode slowly, keeping to the trees as much as he could. A few miles into the canyon showed why the Navajos were so secure in this rocky fortress. Canyons branched off confusingly in all directions.

Which route had Broken Finger and his raiding party taken? Fargo could figure it out, but he had to abandon his stealthy ways to study the trail. He dismounted and rested his Ovaro, thinking hard about what he was doing. This was crazy, something he would have laughed at doing had Chapman ordered him to scout the Navajo stronghold. That it was his own idea made it even more loco.

Knocking the dust from his hat, he mopped at sweat on his forehead, then studied the high canyon rims. The ragged stone up there could hide any number of sentries. Or none at all. Not knowing wore on his nerves worse than if he had spotted a dozen howling, screaming braves all intent on sending him to ride on the Ghost Pony. He wished he had a pair of field glasses, but the only ones he had seen at Fort Fauntleroy belonged to the captain, who never loaned them to anyone else. Still, his sharp eyes picked out several spots where Navajos might sit and watch for any invasion.

Not only whites but Zuñis and the other Pueblos were possibly inclined to chase after raiders. Again Fargo tried to work out why he had embarked on such a crazy chase. What if he did catch Broken Finger? Then what? He would never be able to waltz out of Canyon de Chelly with a prisoner. And Fargo was no assassin. He fought and fought well, but did it honorably. Moreover, just killing Broken Finger accomplished nothing but causing more bad blood. There would be another—a dozen, maybe more—braves willing to take the place of a foully murdered, esteemed clan member and avenge his death.

The only answer Fargo had was that this might be his best chance to stop a part of the trouble in northwestern New Mexico Territory. If the Navajos stopped their raiding, only the troubles between the Pueblos, whites, and Mexicans remained. Fargo considered the matter a moment and wondered how much of that could be laid at Austin Kincaide's feet. Selling Taos Lightning was a risky way of making money. The customers tended to get violent and turn on the gent selling the firewater. If he was indeed selling the moonshine, Kincaide couldn't be helping matters any.

The sun set fast behind the western rim, giving a curiously yellow tint almost like butterscotch to the very air. The quality of the light was something Fargo had never seen before. It was almost as if an insubstantial fog now floated along the canyons. He took advantage of the crazy light to hurry to the trail and study it. Now and then he looked up, hoping to spot a sentry outlined against the twilight sky before they spotted him.

He saw nothing—but he did find Broken Finger's trail. Fargo looked up the straight canyon leading due north. Wherever that trail led, Broken Finger had taken it many times before. Fargo saw no indication of hesitation on the Navajo chief's part. In several instances, Broken Finger's band had taken shortcuts off the trail, showing they were intimately familiar with the terrain. Fargo walked along briskly, his horse shielding him from direct observation from the east. He knew this was not good enough if he was spotted by a sharp-eyed brave, either on that rim or the one to the west. It was the best he could do for the moment, keeping him close to the ground with the tracks he had to follow and as anonymous as he could make himself.

A grassy meadow presented Fargo with his first problem. Hogans dotted the broad expanse, with women and children running around outside of them. All the doors opened east, according to Navajo custom. Fargo made use of this to cut south, hoping to avoid being noticed.

The cooking fires provided small oases of light in the darkness. Bleating sheep and the occasional lowing of cattle interrupted the otherwise peaceful evening. Fargo found himself lulled into a sense of security by the dark and the conventional surroundings. It was so peaceful.

The large group of Navajos took Fargo by surprise.

He came out from a small stand of piñon pines and found himself staring at a knot of Navajos easily topping forty men. Among them were several warriors astride their ponies, riding as if they had been born mounted.

Fargo knew better than to make any sudden moves that might draw their attention. He slowed his progress, letting the band pass along at a slightly quicker pace. Drifting back toward the stand of trees allowed him to find deep shadow. He heaved a sigh of relief when he regained the shelter of the piñons. Watching carefully, Fargo wondered what was going on. A mile or two across the broad, grassy meadow he saw two more groups of Navajos. All headed west, into a branching canyon filled with peach trees and dotted with what he took to be crops.

Fargo scratched his head, wondering what was going on. He had always heard the Navajos were marauders, drifters who raided and stole what they needed. But farmers? Fruit trees by the row? Canyon de Chelly held many mysteries he had no time to delve into. Fargo wondered how he was going to pluck Broken Finger out from the center of such a huge gathering of the clans.

For it was obvious to him that more than one clan was on the move. He recognized members of the Red House, Bitter Water, and Under His Cover clans. Then Fargo frowned because coming down the road he had followed into the meadow was another clan grouping— the Poles Strung Out clan from over Chaco way. Whatever event was going on, it was big enough to draw Navajos from such a distance. Politics among the clans was a mystery to him, but Fargo thought many did not get along too well. That so many met in the heart of the Navajo stronghold was important information Chapman needed.

He hesitated about backtracking and getting out of

Canyon de Chelly. Fargo had it in his head to snatch Broken Finger away and use him as a hostage to force the Navajos into a peace treaty. That was as wild a notion as any he had ever gotten, but perhaps it was more important to abandon it to tell Chapman of this meeting of so many diverse and distant members of the *Dinéh*, "The People," as the Navajo called themselves.

Fargo mounted but rode parallel to the clans marching to the west, trying to stay out of sight as much as he could but finding the chore difficult in the dark.

Fargo blundered onto the Navajo brave before he even saw him. The Ovaro did a quick crow-hop and avoided stepping on the sleeping man, but the action brought the Navajo warrior upright, knife in hand.

Before the Navajo could cry out, Fargo launched himself from astride the horse. His shoulder crashed into the Navajo's chest, driving the man back flat onto the ground. The odor of liquor caused Fargo's nostrils to flare. The brave was drunk and had come out into the woods to sleep it off.

Fargo grabbed a brawny wrist and forced the brave's knife around, the tip pointed at the man's chest. Seeing his predicament caused the Navajo to sober up fast. With a surge of power, he lifted Fargo and threw him to the ground. Fargo came to his feet fast, but the Indian was faster. He lit out running, hollering at the top of his lungs.

"Come back here," growled Fargo, knowing the Navajo could not hear him. He put his head down, and he began running after his fleeing foe. Legs pumping hard, Fargo overtook the Navajo just before he burst out into plain view of a dozen members of the Red Forehead clan.

Arms circling the brave's legs, Fargo brought him down. The Navajo tried to fight, but Fargo was too determined not to be found out. A hard fist crashed into the Navajo's face, breaking his nose and causing him intense pain. He tried to fight back, but Fargo caught the hand holding the knife and turned it around. This time the Navajo did not escape. Fargo killed him with his own knife, plunging it into his chest.

Panting from the exertion of the fight, Fargo sat back and stared at the dead warrior. If he had not been drunk, Fargo wouldn't have stood a chance against him. But then if he hadn't been drunk, he would not have been sleeping in the middle of a poorly traveled trail meandering through a scrubby forest.

Fargo grabbed the man under the arms and dragged him deeper into the woods, leaving him covered by a few fallen tree limbs. The dried brown needles still on the dead branches did little to hide the body, but Fargo didn't plan on being in Canyon de Chelly long enough for it to matter. All hell would be out for lunch when the body was found.

He caught his Ovaro and rode faster now, feeling a sense of urgency. To his right were enough Navajos to kill him a thousand times over. Being in the heart of their territory, at the center of their power, filled him with a curious mixture of wariness and elation.

Fargo reined back when he saw a huge fire blazing ahead, in the middle of a meadow that stretched off into the night. He had the feeling of being in a special place, one devoted to something more than simply growing crops or raising sheep.

He tethered his horse and advanced on foot, curious about the ceremony in progress. Hunkering down, a huge boulder at his back for protection, he watched as the ceremonies began. A medicine man began an intricate chant. After a while Fargo realized he was witnessing a ceremony he had only heard about. This was a Blessing Way sing, one that would span a week or more with nightly rituals. During the day there would be socializing between the clans.

While not always the case, a Blessing Way often was given to protect the warriors before they rode into battle. The Navajos were raiders rather than fighters, but no one crossed them when they got their dander up.

Fargo was watching the beginning of a war. What he did not know was the enemy. Utes? The Pueblos? *Los ricos?* The white settlers? Anyone and everyone who was not Navajo? He had no idea.

What he did know was that Broken Finger walked

among others much older, speaking earnestly and occasionally sitting with them to smoke. Fargo had seen politicians in Denver City and other big towns when they wanted to get elected. That was how Broken Finger acted now, moving from one clan leader to another.

The chant grew in intensity, and Broken Finger joined the others in the ceremony, taking part with hundreds of Navajos. Fargo considered the likelihood of the sing lasting far into the night. Sooner or later, Broken Finger had to leave the others. When he did, Fargo would nab him.

Then it might get really interesting. Until then, Fargo had nothing to do but sit and watch and try to make sense out of the ceremony. Not understanding much Navajo, that proved hard. He started drifting to sleep, lulled by the singsong chant. He snapped erect when the music suddenly stopped.

Cursing under his breath, he got to his feet and circled the clearing, hoping he had not lost Broken Finger in the crowd. He finally spotted the war chief, mounting a horse to return to his hogan, wherever that might be.

Fargo judged distances and his luck, then forgot about anything but capturing the chief. Feet pounding, Fargo ran alongside the dirt track where Broken Finger rode slowly. He climbed fast, scrambling to the top of a rock, and launched himself through the air. For a fleeting instant, Fargo felt as if he had taken wing.

Then he collided with Broken Finger and was brought harshly back to reality. The pair crashed to the ground, Fargo on top. The Navajo had the wind knocked from his lungs, and this gave Fargo the edge. If only for a few seconds.

He knocked the knife from Broken Finger's feeble grip, then saw how the Indian had come to be named. The little finger on his right hand had been broken and misset, healing so that it jutted out at a bizarre angle. Then Fargo was past figuring out such things because the chief recuperated enough to kick out. His moccasined foot expertly caught Fargo high on the thigh, sending a lance of pain into his leg and bringing him down to one knee as the muscle spasmodically jerked.

Broken Finger tried to punch, but Fargo avoided it. He realized the fight had to end fast, before Broken Finger got his strength back or another of the Navajos noticed what was going on. Fargo fell forward, his elbow crashing down into the middle of Broken Finger's chest. Again the air gushed from tortured lungs, and the Navajo was left thrashing about weakly.

This time Fargo wasted no time in using his own knife to cut a long, thin piece of rawhide from Broken Finger's ornately decorated leather shirt. He whipped it around the man's wrists like he was hog-tying a calf for branding. Then he took his own bandanna and stuffed it into the Indian's gaping mouth. Broken Finger choked, but Fargo refused to quit until he had the gag securely tied in place with another strip of hide cut from Broken Finger's shirt.

The Navajo's feet slipped on the dirt as Fargo pulled him erect.

"Come on. Make any sound and I'll kill you," he told Broken Finger in a cold voice.

The Navajo's eyes widened when he got his first good look at Fargo. He recognized Fargo as the man who had aided him and the young slaves go free at the Zuñi encampment. That surprise of recognition turned to sullenness. He moved with all the grace of a bull elk with a broken leg, forcing Fargo to shove him along.

"No dawdling," Fargo warned. "I don't want to kill you, but I will if you warn any of the others."

Fargo knew the threat was meaningless to both of them. He was no more likely to kill a bound, unarmed man than Broken Finger was to cooperate like a docile sheep.

Getting Broken Finger's horse proved harder than capturing the Navajo chief. But Fargo succeeded and dumped the chief unceremoniously belly-down over the horse's rounded back. He walked alongside, wary of Broken Finger trying to slip over the horse and get away using his mount as a diversion.

"All right, get on so we can ride," Fargo told the Indian after he retrieved his Ovaro. Swinging up easily into the saddle, Fargo stared down at his bound captive and saw how difficult that might be. Broken Finger looked as if he wanted to take his chances trying to get away, but for some reason he hesitated. That was enough for Fargo. He bent low, grabbed Broken Finger by the upper arms, and heaved mightily, lifting him off the ground. The Navajo's legs scissored over his horse as he settled down. He glared at Fargo but made no move to escape.

Fargo realized how harebrained his scheme was. He could not ride into the heart of Navajo power and kidnap one of their favorite war chiefs. Yet he had, and without being seen so far. A cold lump settled in his gut when he realized that the easy part was over.

Here on out, it got hard. Damned hard.

"Ride," he ordered. Broken Finger put his heels to his horse's sides and trotted off, Fargo right behind him.

One mistake and he was dead. A new wave of cold caused Fargo to shiver when he realized death might be preferable to what the Navajos would do to him if he got caught.

It had been only a few miles into Canyon de Chelly. It seemed like a thousand getting out.

8

Fargo relaxed a mite when he and Broken Finger came
to the narrow mouth of Canyon de Chelly. He had re-
traced his earlier trip in only a couple of hours, never
stopping and certainly not giving in to the muffled grunts
and half-understood threats Broken Finger uttered
through the gag in his mouth.

He checked the wheeling stars above and saw it was
getting toward dawn, although pink fingers of light had
yet to caress the eastern sky. Riding in a high-walled
canyon had its drawbacks, such as not being able to see
the horizon and get a view of more than just a slice of
sky above. Fargo knew he had to go to ground soon
and rest their horses, but not yet. Not until the Navajo
stronghold was well behind him.

As he started out, the sheer canyon walls slowly sinking into the rugged terrain on either side, Fargo felt a
curious sensation he knew better than to ignore. Sometimes he thought it was like someone walking on his
grave. At other times, he dismissed it as an overactive
imagination. But he dared not ignore the feeling of im-
pending disaster now, not with hundreds of Navajo warriors at his back.

Swinging about in the saddle, he craned his neck and
stared up at the canyon rims, first to the west, then to
the east. The dawn he had wondered about now cast a
single ray of pearly light along the easternmost rim of
Canyon de Chelly—outlining a Navajo lookout.

They had been spotted. The distinctive markings on
the Ovaro made it stand out like a sore thumb amid the
thick mat of dark green vegetation all around them. This

dun on snowy white coloration was why the cavalry refused to use the sturdy horses. They were too easy to spot in situations like this.

"Ride," he ordered his captive. He put his heels into the Ovaro's flanks but quickly jerked back on the reins, causing the horse to dig in its hooves. A fountain of dirt shot into the cold morning air, and Fargo saw how Broken Finger had slid from horseback and was running for the distant canyon wall. He loped along, clumsy with his hands bound behind his back and his breathing restricted because of the gag, but the Navajo chief still covered ground fast.

Fargo was faster. His pony shot forward like a Fourth of July rocket after the fleeing Indian. As he drew nearer, Broken Finger began to dodge. It didn't do him any good. Fargo bent low and snared a dangling braid of the Navajo's coarse black hair. Jerking hard, he snapped the Indian's head back and took Broken Finger's feet out from under him, dumping him hard onto his back.

"Don't do that again or I *will* shoot you," Fargo said. He glanced up at the distant canyon rim and knew the worst. The sentry had passed along the word that an army scout had caught one of their most respected leaders. It didn't take a mountain man of any skill to know why the ground shook like it did.

Mounted Navajos were coming. Fast.

Fargo got Broken Finger back onto his horse. The Navajo would ride. Fargo saw that much, but the real question was how far his horse would carry him. The horse wobbled from fatigue; Fargo's was hardly in better condition after the long ride without much rest.

He headed for an arroyo, then followed smaller branches, eventually heading back toward Canyon de Chelly. Broken Finger looked at him curiously, wondering if his captor had finally gone plumb loco. But Fargo knew the pursuing Navajos would lose the trail in the rocky wash, then assume he had lit out in a beeline for Fort Fauntleroy. That would take them far away.

If he kept going this way, he would end up back in the middle of their stronghold. Fargo saw the only alternative was to go due west, bypassing the canyon mouth. If he rode in a wide circle toward the south, he would find a stretch of deadly land called the *malpais* by the Mexicans. The badlands. He had never gone directly through its center but knew firsthand how lethal even the fringes could be. No water, scant vegetation, the only animals thriving there being sidewinders and scorpions.

Fargo pushed the pace until he began wobbling in the saddle from exhaustion, then headed due south. An hour later, he halted and stared ahead. There was no question as to what lay in front of them.

The land had been raped, then burned. Black lava rock strewn all over made the way dangerous for horses' hooves, but the deep ravines and the way a few pathetic creosote bushes struggled to survive in the crevices told Fargo they had quite a ride ahead.

He glanced over his shoulder, considering doubling back. Then he heaved a deep breath. Death in the *malpais* was better than letting the Navajos catch him now.

"I'll take out the gag if you'll keep a civil tongue in your head," Fargo said to Broken Finger. The Navajo chief glared, then nodded once. Fargo had to use his Arkansas toothpick to cut the rawhide strip. It had become damp from Broken Finger's spit, then dried and tightened. Cuts on the sides of his mouth showed how painful it must have been.

"Sorry about that, but I couldn't have you calling out to your friends."

"They are my clan," Broken Finger said. "But what would you know? I can read it in your eyes. You have no family. You are alone."

"Always was, reckon I always will be," Fargo agreed. "You know any watering holes out there?"

"No."

"Then we're both going to get mighty thirsty before we see Fort Fauntleroy," Fargo said. He had regained some strength, and the break had given his Ovaro a chance to recuperate from the frantic escape. The horse Broken Finger rode was struggling, but had heart. It wouldn't quit anytime soon. Fargo wanted to get a few miles into the *malpais* before resting further.

Best of all would be to find water and take a nice, long drink. Even alkali-laced water that was so common in these parts would go down good, if he had a chance to boil out the minerals. Keeping the horses from drinking might be harder.

"Why are you doing this?" asked Broken Finger. "You have no family. There is no reason to kill me."

"No family," Fargo admitted, "but Captain Chapman hired me to do a job. This is my way of doing it."

"By killing me?"

"By making you see it isn't doing anyone any good raiding and taking slaves. Everyone's going to live together out here, one way or another. The sooner you see that and stop raiding and taking slaves, the quicker my job will be done."

"They steal *our* children and women! The Zuñis, the Mexicans, even the Americans. You are all our enemies."

"I can't argue too much on that point, but there's got to be an end to it. You're the best place to start."

Broken Finger cocked his head to one side and peered at Fargo curiously. "You are a strange man. This is not your fight. You tell me the white-eyes captain only pays you. There is no blood feud to wage?"

"None."

Broken Finger worked on this until Fargo found a small sandy spit near what probably was a torrentially running river during spring runoffs. Now it was merely free of gravel and small rocks, affording a comfortable place to spread his blanket.

How he wished it were spring! He could drink every drop of runoff cascading this way.

Fargo made sure his prisoner was securely tied and then dropped off to a troubled sleep, one cursed with dreams of heat and thirst. He was not sure how long he slept but Fargo came awake just as the sun was dipping low in the west. It took him a few seconds to realize he had slept away the day. His mouth was cottony and his belly rumbled from lack of food. He glanced at Broken Finger, who sat in stony silence. Checking the Navajo's bonds, he saw dried blood where Broken Finger had tried to cut himself free by rubbing the rawhide strip against a rock. All he had succeeded in doing was abrading his own flesh.

"I'll get some dinner for us," Fargo said. He did not expect a reply from Broken Finger and didn't get one. Fargo set off and bagged two scrawny rabbits within a few minutes of putting his mind to the hunt. He returned, wondered if he ought to start a fire, then did so. Eating raw rabbit meat was not too smart. He knew enough men who had died from rabbit fever.

He cooked the rabbits, then offered one to Broken Finger. The Navajo hesitated, as if considering how weak he might appear to a white man by eating. Then good sense kicked in and he accepted. Fargo tied Broken Finger's left hand to his right ankle. Given time he could slip free, but Fargo would see it and stop him.

As they ate in silence, Fargo wondered about what he had seen in Canyon de Chelly.

"That was a Blessing Way ceremony, wasn't it?"

Broken Finger looked up sharply, his eyes wild. Then he calmed down and nodded.

"It was a special chant, a Chief Blessing Way."

It was Fargo's turn to nod. He had heard of them and suspected he had snatched Broken Finger away from a tribe ready to proclaim him war chief. Warriors could not openly petition for chief but they could get others to speak for them. That was why Broken Finger had seemed to be flitting from one group to another. He was garnering support so the men of the tribe would vote him their chief. It was unseemly for him to ask openly for the position but it was expected of him to accept if chosen.

Broken Finger had obviously wanted to be chief.

"What's going to happen now that you're with me?" asked Fargo, trying to skirt the issue and not come right out and say how dumb the Navajo must look to the rest of the braves, being kidnapped in the middle of Canyon de Chelly by a lone white man.

"Another will become chief," Broken Finger said. "Perhaps Manuelito. You have done your people no good by keeping me from being chief. He is a firebrand, a wild man who will fight until no one is left standing. Manuelito is a brave man and will make a fierce chief."

"Manuelito," mused Fargo, trying to remember. "He's the tall one? Six foot high and scowls a lot?"

From Broken Finger's grunted response, he knew he was right. Fargo wiped his fingers clean in the sand, then went to find something to drink. With only a canteen between them, they wouldn't last a day out in the *malpais*.

Fargo asked, "You know any watering holes nearby?" He did not expect Broken Finger to tell the truth but wanted to see the Navajo's reaction. His slight frown told Fargo that this was foreign territory for his captive. That made surviving even more difficult.

He tied up the Navajo again, then set out on foot, looking for cactus big enough to provide juicy pulp. Fargo hated eating barrel cactus and prickly pears because of their bitter taste, but a bad taste in the mouth was better than dying of thirst. He found a fishhook cactus to cut open and then took a few pads from a prickly pear back to his prisoner. Broken Finger sucked on them in silence.

Fargo stretched, studied the sky, and saw the constellations he needed to guide himself through this trackless land. Too many men entered the badlands and lost their bearings. Invariably, following their trails, he saw how they curled to the right, travelling in circles and never knowing it up until the moment of their deaths.

"Let's ride," he told Broken Finger. The Indian looked as if he was going to fight but instead turned sullen. Fargo was not sure he preferred this over open rebellion, but getting out of this hell on earth mattered more than what Broken Finger might feel or think of him.

They rode steadily, not pushing their horses. Fargo was careful to let his Ovaro pick its own path through the jagged lava rocks so it wouldn't break a leg or cut itself on the sharp edges. Occasionally checking his position by the stars, he kept a southerly course until almost sunup, then cut due east. This ought to bring them out of the badlands and almost drop them on the doorstep of Fort Fauntleroy.

"I want to get this settled," Fargo said. "There's too much going on that needs some real attention."

"What are you talking about? You take me to the fort to be hanged," Broken Finger said.

"You might deserve it, but that's not why you're going to talk to Captain Chapman. I want you to come to a peace agreement. A treaty so you'll stop your raiding and let the cavalry concentrate on keeping the peace."

"The horse soldiers would fight the Mexicans and Pueblos if we declare a truce?" Broken Finger sounded incredulous.

"Why not? There's going to be peace here one way or the other. Some folks, especially the white settlers in Ojo del Oso, think there's nothing quite so peaceful as a dead Indian."

"You're not one of them," Broken Finger said. Before Fargo could answer, the Navajo chief spat. "You want only to take slaves."

"I don't know where you got that idea, but it's dead wrong," Fargo answered, not trying to keep the heat from his voice. It angered him that Broken Finger thought he was a slave trader.

"You work with the other white-eyes to steal our women and children, then sell them to the Mexicans."

"I let loose a passel of your children from Benavidez's hacienda," Fargo said. "And you know I helped you get that boy free from the Zuñis. What was he to you? Your son?"

"Nephew," Broken Finger answered. "You know that."

"How could I?"

"Because you and the others have stolen away my son. I have no brothers to rescue him. His uncles were all killed by the slavers when they stole him."

"You know what the raiders looked like?"

Broken Finger said nothing for some time. "You are not lying? You turn loose slaves?"

"Can't abide slavery, no matter who's in chains,"

Fargo said simply. The honesty in his voice caused Broken Finger to pause and reflect some more.

"I do not know the identity of the men who stole away Shaking Leaf."

"Shaking Leaf's your boy?"

Broken Finger nodded curtly.

"Tell me what you can about the men who kidnapped Shaking Leaf, and I promise you I'll do what I can to track them down and get your son back."

"Do this and I will talk peace," Broken Finger said.

"Seems fair," Fargo said. "Did you see the men?"

"Only one. A man dressed in fine clothing but with darting dark eyes, as if he were a snake fighting for his life. Thin teeth, again like a snake's fangs. And white skin. Very white as if it had been painted."

Fargo thought about the description. It sounded as if Broken Finger described someone who did not see the light of day but who had a fair amount of money to spend on clothing.

Like a gambler.

Fargo described Jack Sawyer the best he could from seeing him the one time in the Silver Centavo Saloon.

"This might be the one," Broken Finger said, not excited enough to make Fargo think he had hit the bull's-eye. "I cannot say from your description. Show me the man and I will know. Give him to me and I will find out what he has done with my son!"

Fargo decided it wouldn't do to get between Broken Finger and whoever had taken his son. If it was Luella Kincaide's betrothed, Fargo certainly did not envy him.

First, he had to get back to Fort Fauntleroy. With luck and some fresh water, they might make it another day. Somehow, Fargo thought luck was decidedly coming in his direction—and for a change, it was all good.

9

"They will kill me," Broken Finger said, lifting his chin and indicating the dust cloud moving across their trail ahead.

Fargo knew he was likely to be included in that killing spree if *los ricos* caught up with him. First Broken Finger would die, then him. After turning loose all of Benavidez's potential slaves, Fargo knew he had no standing with the Mexicans. At least not with the rancheros like Benavidez and Villanueva.

"Think they might be the ones who kidnapped your boy?" Fargo asked.

Broken Finger said nothing but the set to his shoulders and the way his lips thinned into a line told Fargo it was possible, but the Navajo chief did not think *los ricos* were responsible.

He remembered the description Broken Finger had given of the man who had kidnapped his son. The more Fargo thought about it, the more the culprit sounded like Jack Sawyer. But he had to be sure before accusing the man.

"Benavidez's land butts up against the *malpais*," Fargo said. "We have to cross it to get to Fort Fauntleroy."

"They will kill me. Let me have a knife so I can take my own life—after I have killed many of them."

"I can't do that," Fargo said, aware that Broken Finger considered his life forfeit now if he offered to kill himself. "We'll get by them."

He was not certain how he would do that but so far luck had been with him. They had found a water hole with passable water in it the day before. This had helped them along more than anything else, giving the horses strength and instilling in Fargo the hope that they could get out of the badlands fast. And they had, only to find the way blocked by vaqueros.

Fargo considered everything he had seen. Broken Finger assumed these were Benavidez's riders. It was logical to believe this, since Benavidez's land stretched as far as the eye could see, but Fargo did not know for certain. Those might be soldiers from the fort on patrol. Or one of the inevitable wagon trains moving through to find unclaimed land on which to settle.

In his gut, Fargo knew they were Benavidez's vaqueros and should be avoided. He cut to the north, intending to get around the riders. He cursed when he saw more dust, coming right at him. Craning his neck, he looked back along the trail he and Broken Finger had just ridden. They had come to the edge of the lava rock-strewn *malpais* and he was not inclined to go back. Better to fight it out.

Or go to ground and let the vaqueros ride past.

"Down," Fargo said, coming to a quick decision. "We'll let them find us."

Broken Finger sneered. He was a Navajo, a self-styled Lord of New Mexico, and not inclined to hide unless it meant he was readying himself for an ambush. Fargo knew better than to take on a half-dozen angry vaqueros after all he had done to Benavidez. His only regret was that Chapman had been forced to release the man rather than sending him to the territorial prison where the ranchero belonged.

Fargo led his Ovaro into a rocky cul-de-sac, knowing the trouble he would find himself in if he had to fight. Although the rocks protected him on three sides, it also meant he could not leave unless he killed everyone in the bottleneck. From the sour expression on Broken Finger's face, Fargo could see that the Navajo did not like the situation, either. For the first time, Fargo considered giving the chief his knife back.

The clicking of shod hooves against the lava rock alerted him. Fargo put his finger to his lips to caution

Broken Finger to remain silent. The Navajo sank down to the ground and waited, his dark eyes fixed on Fargo. Taking his Henry from the saddle sheath, Fargo made his way to the narrow entrance to what might prove their burial ground.

He crouched and waited when he heard voices. The first one called out in Spanish. The reply came in English. Fargo thought he knew the voice but was not sure. Behind him Broken Finger let out a yelp, forced his way to his feet, and dashed forward.

"Get down!" But Fargo saw his order wasn't going to be obeyed. As Broken Finger ran past, Fargo shoved his rifle between the Indian's legs, bringing him down hard. Fargo swarmed over Broken Finger and held him face-down on the ground, his knees on the chief's shoulders so he could not move.

"It's him!" grated out Broken Finger.

"Who?"

"The one who took my son! I must kill him!"

"Be quiet," Fargo said, not moving to let up the Navajo. "Stay here and I'll see what's going on. We can't fight them all."

"I'll kill him!" repeated Broken Finger.

"Do that and you'll never find your boy," Fargo said. "Now shut up or I'll slug you."

Broken Finger subsided. Fargo waited a moment until he saw the Navajo was going to obey, then got off him. He jerked his head back toward the horses. Broken Finger's bared teeth made Fargo think he might attack foolishly, but he spun about and stormed away.

Fargo duck-walked forward, using the rocks to shelter himself from view. His eyes went wide when he saw what was going on not twenty feet from the narrow entrance into the cul-de-sac. A dozen vaqueros sat astride their horses while Benavidez stood facing a smirking Texas Jack Sawyer.

"Heard tell you've had a bit of trouble, Señor Benavidez," the gambler drawled. "Heard that Skye Fargo let loose all your carefully chained slaves, the ones that were going to Perez down Sonora way."

"Your ears are like jugs, Sawyer," snapped Benavidez. "They stick out and hear too much."

"You don't want to go insulting me, señor," Sawyer said, his grin widening. "You need me more than ever."

"I need more slaves quickly. Perez is not an understanding *patrón*," Benavidez said, his voice grim. "He has already sold them to others deeper in Mexico."

"Now that could pose a problem for you," Sawyer said. "It's a good thing I got twenty prime boys and girls for you."

"Twenty!"

"Yep," Sawyer said, enjoying the ranchero's surprise. "I've been a busy bee, finding them. Age up to, oh, I'd say twelve or thirteen. None older, so you won't have much trouble with them."

"Navajos?"

Sawyer shrugged. "Some. Some Zuñis, too. I got them at each other's throats. Always stirring the pot, you see, to make it easier to pick up the children when I need them most."

"Navajo, Zuñi, it does not matter."

"Naw, reckon it doesn't, señor," said Sawyer. "They're all heathens. What does it matter?" His sarcasm fell on deaf ears. Fargo saw how Benavidez ignored the gambler. His mind seemed to race, considering how to cheat Sawyer out of the potential slaves and get them to his buyer down in the interior of Mexico.

"How much do you want?"

"Now that's a matter of some discussion, señor," Sawyer said. "I found getting them to be a tad more expensive than usual. Why, one of them might even be a navajo chief's son."

Benavidez waved his hand in dismissal. "What does it matter who plows the fields or picks the corn? You will not cheat me."

"I'm pointing out why these will cost you more." Sawyer looked up as two vaqueros slid pistols from their holsters. "Now, don't go having them do anything you'll regret." Sawyer pointed to the armed riders. "I know where I have the Injuns stashed. You don't. Shoot me down—or just piss me off—and you'll never find 'em."

"Where else would you sell such merchandise?" asked Benavidez.

"You'd be surprised," Sawyer answered. "You're not the only buyer for human flesh out here. But I like you, Señor Benavidez," the gambler hastily added when he saw the ranchero bristle. "That's why I'm giving you first crack at them."

Fargo's finger tensed on the trigger of his Henry. He could take out this foul creature with a single shot. The second bullet would remove Benavidez forever. But Fargo knew he could never outfight the vaqueros backing up the ranchero. More than this, he and Benavidez were in the same position of not knowing where Sawyer had the children hidden.

If Fargo wanted to save them, he had to take Sawyer alive so he could make him talk. And confess.

Jail was too good for some men. Sawyer and Benavidez were two who ought to be strung up from the limb of the nearest cottonwood tree.

"When can you get them to me?" asked Benavidez.

"Not so fast, señor," said Sawyer, obviously warming to the power he had over the ranchero. "We got to come to a deal first. How much you willing to go for each kid?"

"The same. One hundred dollars."

"No, no, I *told* you. I explained these cost me more. If I don't get two hundred—" Sawyer sized up his buyer, judged his mounting rage at being cheated, then changed his tactics. "Make it one-fifty for an old friend and good customer. But I can't go lower than that. After all, I got expenses."

Benavidez balled his hands as if he wanted to strike Sawyer. The gambler never noticed.

"One hundred fifty dollars," Benavidez agreed.

"In gold. I don't want any of that worthless scrip you been passing around."

"It is backed by the Bank of Santa Fé," protested Benavidez.

"Gold," insisted Sawyer. "You'll get me gold. Three thousand dollars' worth of it, but I'm going to make it easy on you."

"How?"

"You can give me either coins or gold dust." Sawyer laughed at Benavidez' outrage at being used like this. "I'll let you know where to leave the gold so I can check it."

"You do not trust me," Benavidez accused.

"Of course not, señor," Sawyer answered.

For a moment, the two stood nose to nose. Then Benavidez laughed. Sawyer thrust out his hand and the ranchero shook it reluctantly.

"By the end of the week. I must have the slaves transported south by the end of the week."

"You'll get 'em, señor," Sawyer promised. "Good doing business with you."

Texas Jack Sawyer swung into the saddle, touched the brim of his bowler, then wheeled about and trotted off. Fargo watched Benavidez's reaction. The ranchero fought to keep from ordering his vaqueros to shoot the gambler in the back.

Benavidez said something in Spanish that Fargo could not hear, but the vaqueros laughed. Benavidez mounted, glared in Sawyer's direction as he made an obscene gesture, then led his men like a general at the head of a conquering army. Again, Fargo considered a single shot but Benavidez quickly vanished, heading east onto the grassy land that formed the western section of his vast ranch.

Fargo heaved a sigh, then relaxed. He had not realized how taut his nerves had become listening to the illicit deal in human flesh being made. Keeping a low profile, he made his way back into the cul-de-sac to find Broken Finger again trying to cut through the rawhide strips binding his wrists.

Fargo said nothing as he checked to see how far the Navajo had gotten. More blood from chafed wrists soaked into the rawhide, but the thong was still sturdy enough to restrain Broken Finger.

"Mount up. We got a passel of miles to ride," Fargo said, not commenting on the Navajo's new attempts to escape. He did not say anything to Broken Finger about what he had overheard, either. The chief might take it into his head to go after Jack Sawyer on his own. If Fargo wanted the bloodshed to stop in this part of New Mexico Territory, he had to take out the key players himself.

Stopping Broken Finger's raids was a good start.

Taking out Benavidez and Texas Jack Sawyer would be even more satisfying.

"I don't believe it," Captain Chapman said after listening to Fargo's report. "No white man's ever gotten out of Canyon de Chelly alive, much less after snatching one of their fiercest warriors."

Fargo had not mentioned the Chief Blessing Way sing that would have selected Broken Finger as their war chief.

"Reckon Broken Finger just came out of his own free will, then," Fargo said dryly.

"I'm sorry, Fargo," said Chapman. "This is so incredible, and you make it sound so easy. I was joking before when I said there'd be peace in the territory if I had a dozen men like you. Now, it looks as if all I need is one—*you.*"

"You're giving me too much credit," Fargo said. "Keep Broken Finger under wraps for a while so I can look into some things he told me. If I can clear them up, you might negotiate a treaty with the Navajos that'll free up most of your cavalry troopers."

"Amazing, simply amazing," Chapman said, shaking his head in amazement.

"Any luck finding the boys I freed from Benavidez's shed?" Fargo asked.

"None. It's as if the earth opened up and swallowed them whole. But I don't think they'll be needed."

"Why not? You have other evidence on Benavidez?"

"No, not that. I think Benavidez will walk the straight and narrow path from now on. He doesn't want to risk losing his rancho, hacienda, and everything else he has by selling slaves."

"You get this straight from the horse's mouth?"

"Benavidez? No, not exactly. But Villanueva said that *los ricos* will do what they can to stop the slave trade.

He said they recognize how it is dangerous for all concerned."

Fargo said nothing about overhearing Sawyer making the deal with Benavidez. *Los ricos* were lying to the captain, and he was swallowing it hook, line, and sinker.

"Watch Benavidez awhile longer," Fargo said. "See if he tries to get in a shipment of gold."

"Gold?"

"About three thousand dollars' worth," Fargo said. Chapman was puzzled but Fargo was not going to enlighten him. He preferred to deliver the twenty children to testify against both Sawyer and Benavidez without the U.S. Army getting in his way.

"Whatever you want, but I can't say I understand," Captain Chapman said.

Fargo left the fort, intent on finding where Texas Jack Sawyer had hidden away his human cargo.

Austin Kincaide's store did a booming business. The man had recovered from his beating but played up his injuries to the fullest, sitting in a chair with one bandaged leg propped up, directing his daughters like a king might his subjects.

Fargo slipped around back and then pressed himself flat against the hot exterior adobe wall when he saw two Pueblo Indians sitting impatiently by the door leading to the back storeroom. At first he thought they only sought shade, but when the sun moved and they were exposed to its searing rays, they still did not move. Fargo knew patience but felt the pressure of time to find Texas Jack Sawyer and the children he had kidnapped. As he started to slip away and leave the Indians to whatever mischief they were up to, he heard the rear door creak open on unoiled hinges.

"There you are," Austin Kincaide said. The man hobbled out, putting more weight on his foot than he could if it had been severely injured. The shopkeeper looked around, then reached inside the back door and pulled out two bottles filled with amber fluid.

Firewater. Taos Lightning. He was selling the illicit booze to the Indians.

They greedily grabbed for the bottles, but Kincaide expertly held them out of reach.

"Not till you pony up some money," Kincaide said.

The two reluctantly handed over their sweat-stained greenbacks. Kincaide tossed them the liquor and slammed the door. The two Indians left hurriedly, clutching their precious firewater as if it were a lifeline and they were drowning. Fargo snorted in disgust. What Luella Kincaide had said about her father was true. He was selling liquor illegally. Fargo did not doubt he also sold to soldiers from Fort Fauntleroy, in direct contradiction of Captain Chapman's orders for abstinence in his command.

Fargo decided to confront Kincaide directly and tell him to stop the liquor trafficking. Before he could get into the store and find the owner, he found himself holding an armful of a delightfully squirming feminine body.

"Skye!" cried Dorothea. "I thought I saw you a few minutes ago. Well, more than that, actually. Where did you go?"

"Around back," he said.

"Whatever for? It's so much cooler in the store." She batted her eyes and let him mentally add that she offered attractions not to be found elsewhere in Ojo del Oso. On that Fargo could not argue, but he wanted to have words with her father.

"I need to—"

"Come with me," she cut in, smoothly finishing his sentence for him. Dorothea took his arm and pulled him away from the store. "Papa is finally feeling his oats again and let me have the afternoon off. He and Lu can handle the customers."

He started to ask if she knew her father was selling Taos Lightning out the back door, then stopped. Something told him Dorothea was innocent of such dealings and to mention it would only hurt her. Better to deal directly with her father, get him to stop and put an end to the entire sordid affair.

"Where are you going?" he asked.

"Where are *we* going is a better question," she said, not letting loose of his arm. "You go running off and I don't see you for days and days. You come back and the first thing you want to do is run off again. Why, a girl might think you found her ugly."

"Never that," Fargo said, grinning. And it was true. Dorothea was gorgeous. She was dressed in a crisp white blouse that threatened to pop open at any moment every time she took a deep breath. A soft brown-dyed cotton dress swayed around her womanly hips as she sashayed along and her long blonde hair had been pulled back and was held with a silver comb that glinted in the sunlight. Most exciting for Fargo, Dorothea's twinkling blue eyes danced with merriment and promised him what he had been missing since he left Ojo del Oso.

"I think it is time for a little siesta. The heat makes everyone drowsy. Everyone but Papa and my sister, that is," Dorothea added with just a trace of bitter feelings.

"You and Luella don't get on very well, do you?"

"I already told you that. She's stuck up and always poking her nose into everyone else's business when she ought to tend her own."

"What about Texas Jack?"

"What about him? He's a lowdown, no-account tinhorn gambler. Other than that, he's cheap, smells of bad cologne and will desert Lu the first chance he gets. I'll be real happy when he gets out of town for a few days. Said he was going to Santa Fé tomorrow, but if I know him, he's already cheating on Lu and he's got another woman stashed somewhere, maybe some squaw."

Fargo noticed Dorothea did not mention "dealer in slaves" among Sawyer's ignoble attributes. She might not know, and he was not going to be the one to tell her.

"You might try getting Luella away from him."

"Make a play for a man like Texas Jack when I have a real stallion in my corral? Whatever are you thinking, Skye?" Dorothea moved a bit closer. Her hand crept around his waist and then lower until she goosed him.

"This stallion's hankering after your corral," he said truthfully. Fargo felt himself responding to her, and it was getting a mite tight at his crotch.

"There, up there," Dorothea said, pointing to a winding trail leading up onto a ridge. "We'll have a good view from there. Real good."

Neither of them was paying a whole lot of attention to the view as they slowly took off items of clothing while they walked. By the time they reached the top of the ridge, which looked out over Ojo del Oso and gave a panorama of Fort Fauntleroy in the distance, Fargo had stripped off his shirt and Dorothea was working to get him out of his buckskins.

"Oh, now *that's* a sight," she said as she freed his manhood from its cloth prison. He jerked erect, and she engulfed him with her lips. Turning her eyes upward, she gave him a wickedly sinful look. Then her mouth began sucking and her tongue lapped at him like a kitten at a saucer of milk. Fargo turned weak in the knees and sank down slowly. Dorothea followed.

As she eagerly worked at his groin, he stripped off the blouse she had unbuttoned on the way up to the top of the hill. She shucked it off and was gloriously naked to the waist. Her breasts bobbed seductively, capped with taut nipples the color of old pennies. Fargo pinched them gently, then gasped when this caused Dorothea to suck even harder on his shaft.

"You're going to pull my innards out that way," he said. The sensations working their way into his loins threatened to rob him of all control. He reached down and cupped her breasts, stroking them and then lifting her up.

Dorothea got the idea and drew back from her hungry gobbling.

"We ought to get in the shade," she said. "It's hot out here, and I don't want you to sunburn your privates." She stroked Fargo's length until he gulped.

"No need to worry about it being in the sun. I intend to put it where it won't see any light."

"And where might that be, Skye?" she coyly asked, settling down on the pile of clothing they had discarded. Using it as a blanket, Dorothea rocked back, drew up her legs, and lifted her skirts out of the way.

Fargo could hardly believe how he responded to her. The sight of paradise being offered so openly excited

77

him even more. He moved into the V formed by her wantonly spread legs. The tip of the organ she had just mouthed brushed across her nether lips. The surge of delight passing through both of them made them gasp in unison.

"So nice, Skye, so nice. But I'm hollow inside. Fill me up. I know you can. You did before. Ohhh!"

He moved forward, holding up his weight on his arms. His hips swept forward and the end of his manhood parted her pink scalloped lips and plunged deep into her steamy interior.

They had gasped before. Now those gasps turned to cries of pure delight. Fargo felt her thighs on either side of his body as she tried to crush him. This only pulled him deeper into her, exciting them both even more.

"Move, oh, yes, so big, so nice, but move! Don't just stand still!"

He levered his hips back until only his tip remained within her, then he shoved forward hard and fast. The carnal heat he generated added a new dimension to the lovemaking. Bending down, he licked and kissed and sucked at her breasts. Then he withdrew from her tightly clutching sheath of female flesh.

"More, Skye, more!"

"Like this?" he asked needlessly. Fargo began a steady, powerful thrusting that gradually sped up until his hips flew. Every time he drilled into her, she let out a tiny gasp of pure pleasure. Then those tiny gasps turned to moans and the moans to cries of ecstasy. All the while, he kept pushing in, hard and deep. He ground his hips around in a powerful circle, then pulled back, only to repeat the motion even faster.

When he felt her inner muscles begin to clench, he knew she was going to get off. This excited him even more. His rhythm turned ragged as he lost control. He was aware of Dorothea screaming out her lust. He was more aware of the way her body clenched down around him as if he had plunged into a velvet-gloved grip. The pressures within and without all collided.

He spilled over in a fast rush, then sank down beside

the woman. They were covered with sweat and he knew the summer sun was not entirely responsible.

"Oh, Skye, you're so good," she cooed. She burrowed closer to him, her cheek on his bare chest. His hand rested on one of Dorothea's breasts. She put her hand over his and began squeezing, giving him the idea she wanted more.

"You're insatiable," he accused.

"I don't know that for a fact. Do you?"

Fargo had to find out. And he did.

10

Fargo stared out over the heat-shimmery Ojo del Oso from the vantage point on the hill above the town. Dorothea lay comfortably beside him, sleeping like a baby in the torrid day. He glanced down at her and smiled. She was an enticing woman, even more so since she had not bothered dressing after their lovemaking. Naked, with tiny beads of sweat dancing on her white skin, she was about the most beautiful sight he had ever seen.

But Fargo kept coming back to what Dorothea had said rather than the woman herself and what they had done together. Jack Sawyer was leaving for Santa Fé tomorrow. After spying on Sawyer's conversation with Benavidez out in the *malpais*, Fargo knew Texas Jack was going to pick up the kidnapped children. Fargo doubted they were in Santa Fé, but were more likely hidden away somewhere in the mountains along the road to the territorial capital. That meant Sawyer had at least one henchman and probably more, since he would not leave the children alone.

Feeding them, seeing they had enough water in this crushing summer heat—these weren't the reasons Sawyer wouldn't leave the children unguarded. The gambler simply did not want his precious treasure in human flesh to escape.

Fargo reached over and put his hand on the woman's bare breast. Dorothea stirred and smiled. She snuggled closer. Fargo stroked over the creamy slope and brushed his finger across her increasingly rigid nipple. Flicking it a few times provoked a purr like that of a contented kitten. She was quite a woman.

Fargo looked back down at Ojo del Oso and the fort beyond, barely visible due to dust hanging in the still air. This town was not the sleepy little village it appeared to be, and the fort was hardly more useful than tits on a bull. Trouble brewed and threatened to boil over at any moment. Dorothea's father sold firewater to the Indians, which undoubtedly provoked them into attacks. The Pueblos raided the Navajos for slaves, just as the Navajos raided their traditional enemies. The whites moved in and settled on land the Mexicans thought theirs by grant from the Spanish king a century and more ago. The poorer Mexicans thought Kincaide and the others in Ojo del Oso cheated them at every turn. Added into the mix were *los ricos,* also trafficking in slaves. Men like Texas Jack Sawyer added to the problem and fanned the flames of anger to the point where there would be open warfare soon.

The Blessing Way sing Fargo had witnessed told him the Navajos were preparing for a war that no one could win. Broken Finger was the best hope for diverting some of that anger and soothing ruffled feathers. To do that, the slave trade had to stop. Completely.

Fargo knew no one would be happy with such a solution, least of all the Navajos. They raided and kidnapped women and children but seemed to absorb them into their clans. That had to be a better fate than being sold to some slaveholder down in Mexico.

But slavery was slavery, no matter what.

When he had agreed to scout for Captain Chapman, he had not thought it would be so involved.

Fargo turned back when Dorothea stirred again. Her blue eyes flickered open, and she smiled more broadly.

"This is the way to wake up," she said dreamily. Dorothea put her hand over Fargo's and pulled it down harder onto her naked breast. "I could get to like this, Skye."

"I have some business out at the fort," he said. "It might take a day or two, but I'll be back then."

"I wish you could stay." Her hands began exploring. Fargo moved away. As much as he would like to share the rest of the day with her, he had to track down Texas Jack and find out where he was really headed.

"Me, too," he said. Fargo hesitated about questioning her about her father's illicit trade in Taos Lightning. And about Luella's relationship with Sawyer. It worried Fargo a mite that Luella might be involved in the slave trade with her fiancé.

"You're mighty quiet all of a sudden. Don't you like me anymore?"

"You said Texas Jack was heading for Santa Fé tomorrow," Fargo said. "Does he go there often?"

"Enough to make Lu upset."

"Does he go hunting, too?"

"Why, yes, a couple times a week." Dorothea snorted in contempt. "He never bags anything. Not even a scrawny little rabbit, but he comes back stinking of black powder like he's been in a gunfight. I don't think he's a very good shot." She sat up and put her blouse on to cover her nakedness, and then peered suspiciously at him. "Why the interest in a lowlife like him?"

"I'm a better hunter. Maybe I can find out where he hunts and bring something big back."

"Why do I get the feeling we're not talking about shooting a deer?"

Fargo smiled, bent over, and kissed her. Dorothea was as quick as she was pretty. But it was time for him to get on Sawyer's trail.

The gambler pushed back his bowler hat and fanned the cards in front of him. Fargo watched the poker game from across the saloon and knew the man was bluffing. He wasn't much for betting on the cards or bucking the tiger at faro, but he knew enough about wagering to see that Texas Jack Sawyer was a piss-poor gambler. But he won enough off the men in the Silver Centavo to keep him in liquor.

When he left, Fargo finished his beer and trailed behind, not wanting to be too obvious. Sawyer strutted down the middle of Ojo del Oso's main street as if he owned it. He paused when he came to the general store. Fargo had looked in earlier and knew Luella was working this evening, giving her pa time off to rest. Fargo half expected Sawyer to go in and Luella to hang out a CLOSED sign.

The gambler kept walking, his stride lengthening as determination set in. This was what Fargo had hoped for. Sawyer was going to fetch the children he had kidnapped.

Sawyer argued with the livery owner over how much he owed, finally settled accounts, then mounted his roan mare and headed out on the road leading to Santa Fé. Fargo let him disappear before going after him, but he kept an eye peeled. The twilight deepened and the quarter moon rising above Mount Taylor was not going to afford much light. It would be easy to miss the trail when Sawyer left the main road.

And Fargo knew the tinhorn gambler would do just that somewhere along the road because he had no business in Santa Fé. His illegal dealings were all with Benavidez.

Even keeping a closer watch, Fargo almost missed where Sawyer cut off the road, heading down into an arroyo and continuing on toward the high country. Fargo dismounted, knelt and studied the tracks. They were fresh. One hoofprint had pressed down firmly into bone-dry dirt, showing a large nick on the horse's front hoof and how the shoe was about ready to fall off. This reinforced Fargo's opinion of Luella Kincaide's betrothed. He cared nothing about tending to his horse, let alone to human lives.

Walking a hundred yards, Fargo assured himself he had the trail. He mounted and walked his Ovaro along slowly, enjoying the chilly evening after the heat of the day. As he rode, his thoughts drifted to Dorothea and Broken Finger and everything that had happened to him since taking the job as Chapman's scout.

He was close to accomplishing everything—and more— that the captain had wanted done. What would he do then? Dorothea Kincaide was a mighty appealing woman and had the wiles to chain a man securely without using shackles.

"Soft fetters," he mused. Before he could explore

what this meant and what he might do about it, he heard a gunshot from up the draw. Fargo grabbed his Henry and crouched to the ground. He made sure his Ovaro was securely tied before advancing on foot.

He had come across Sawyer's hideout far sooner than anticipated. Fargo held back his need to find the cause of the gunshot because he had not scouted the area. If he fell to Sawyer's six-shooter, the children would be doomed to a life of slavery in Mexico.

And all of northwestern New Mexico Territory would explode in a bloody war that would take years to burn out, because Broken Finger's son would be among that group sold down south. Fargo did not need that kind of burden to carry with him to the Happy Hunting Grounds.

"Dang it, Jack," came a whining voice. "The little snot was tryin' to git away!"

"You stupid son of a bitch." Texas Jack Sawyer snarled. "You cost us a hundred dollars!"

"If I hadn't a' plugged him, he'd have gone and let everyone know where we was."

"I ought to—" Sawyer cut off his threat and instead said, "That's all right, Binks. We'll tell Benavidez we had to kill that one because he had the pox."

"Won't he think the others'll be poxy, too?" spoke up a third man.

Fargo wiggled closer, and wedged himself between two rocks and stared into a sandy pit where a fire guttered. He barely made out Sawyer and another man. The third one was beyond his field of vision. Before he took them down, he had to know what he was up against.

"All you do is make problems," Sawyer said angrily. "Let *me* do the thinking. I do it better anyhow."

"Jack, don't go rilin' me like that." The third man stepped into Fargo's vision. With the man was another, a mountain of a man. "You get me mad, you make Pete here awful mad."

"Calm down, all of you. There's no need to get your dander up," Sawyer said, backtracking in an effort to soothe his partners. "We aren't going to pass up this much money, are we? Why, we'll be making almost two hundred dollars apiece.''

Fargo cursed under his breath. That meant Sawyer might have two or three more men with him, even cheating them by claiming a hundred a head instead of the real price Benavidez had agreed to.

"I don't like foolin' round with these Injun kids. They're too much trouble. I want to get back to robbing stagecoaches.''

"How much did we ever make robbing stages?" demanded Sawyer. "Not half as much as we stand to make selling them to Benavidez.'' He jerked his thumb over his shoulder, indicating a spot uphill.

Fargo took this as a sign he ought to let the outlaws argue among themselves while he saw to freeing the children. These owlhoots were lower than a snake's belly in his opinion, preying on kids and selling them like so many head of cattle. He wanted to settle matters with them but knew he might be content with letting the soon-to-be slaves go, just as he had done at Benavidez's hacienda.

Fargo circled around and came upon another small depression in the rocks. He faded into shadow when a burly man sauntered by, a shotgun resting in the crook of his left arm. The man stopped not five feet from Fargo, sniffed the air, then turned and sniffed again.

"What's wrong, Emmitt?" called out a man nearer to the children.

"Cain't rightly say. Smelt somethin', I think.''

"You ain't never had a thought in your life. You see anythin' or not?''

Fargo considered how difficult it would be taking out these two without their partners hearing. It wasn't difficult—it was impossible. The one named Emmitt roved around, but his friend was hidden away where Fargo could not spot him. He had a good idea where the man might be, but if he missed, all hell would be out for lunch.

He dared not fail or the lives of ten or more children would be forfeit. He felt bad enough about the one already shot down trying to escape and that he couldn't do anything about it. Yet.

As he slipped away, heading back to get his horse, Fargo considered the problem from all sides. If Chapman came out with a company of soldiers, Sawyer and the others would probably escape. The cavalry had its own brand of doing things, and sneaking up on a camp filled with slavers was not part of their training. If they circled the camp and ordered Sawyer to give up, he or the other desperadoes with him might begin killing the children.

Fargo needed help getting the children away from Sawyer and his gang, but it was help Chapman was not likely able to provide. Worse, the captain wouldn't take kindly to being told his mandate was worthless in a situation like this. The U.S. Army might fight bravely if they could lay traps and make frontal attacks and sweep along enemy flanks, but Sawyer had mobility, and the cover of darkness.

To save lives and be sure Sawyer was brought to justice required talents to be found at Fort Fauntleroy—but not by any soldier.

"You *what*?" bellowed Chapman. The man had been in bed when Fargo had roused him. He pulled on his military jacket, but this did nothing to lend him an air of authority.

"I know it sounds outrageous, Captain, but you have to trust me on this."

"No! Definitely not. Out of the question."

"You can't rightly hold him," Fargo pressed. "There aren't any charges filed against Broken Finger, are there?"

"He's a Navajo!"

"That might not be looked on too favorably in these parts, but last I heard it wasn't a crime."

"Fargo, this is impossible. I will not release Broken Finger. You were the one who brought him in because you thought he was the cause of all the trouble between the Zuñis and the Navajos, not to mention stirring up *los ricos* and raiding our supply wagons."

"All that's true, Captain, but if I promise that releasing him will put an end to all those woes, then will you sign the order?"

"No. Broken Finger stays in the stockade where he belongs." Chapman finally shook off the last vestiges of sleep and speared Fargo with a steely look. "What's caused this sudden change of heart?"

"I've got a lot of irons in the fire, Captain, and need some expert help with part of it."

"And I and my men are *not* so expert? What are you insinuating?"

"Don't get testy, Captain. I know there's going to be a swap of at least ten slaves on Benavidez's land out at the edge of the *malpais*. I don't know where, and it will take a lot of careful patrolling on your part to find out."

"A wild-goose chase," grumbled Chapman.

The officer calmed down when he saw Fargo's face. The Trailsman was not pulling his leg. This was not a joke, and he could see Fargo did not have the time to explain the details.

"All right, what do you want?"

"Here," Fargo said, pointing out on a map the region of Benavidez's land where he had seen the ranchero meet with Texas Jack Sawyer. "Patrol this area, looking for slavers."

"What will you be doing?"

"Broken Finger and I will—"

"No!" Chapman slammed his fist down on his desk so hard that a book jumped and papers went flying. "That savage stays in the stockade. If I let him out, I'll never see him again—unless I'm sighted down his rifle barrel."

Fargo saw how personally Chapman took the release of Broken Finger. It was as if he was admitting failure if the Navajo chief rode away from Fort Fauntleroy.

"It'll be harder, what I have to do, but I can only do it alone."

"You want to take Sergeant Sallin? He's a good man. Knows all kinds of tribal lore. I used him as scout before you hired on."

Fargo had seen the sergeant and knew he had some skill, but not enough to sneak up on Sawyer's camp and get the children away. Sallin was one of those soldiers best suited to blaring trumpets and full frontal assaults. Brave to a fault, he simply lacked the abilities needed for this rescue.

"You'll need him on your patrol," Fargo said. He knelt and picked up the papers Chapman had scattered. Fargo quickly leafed through them, slipping one under his buckskin shirt before standing up and putting the papers back on the officer's desk.

"Thanks, Fargo," Chapman said. He buttoned his jacket and pulled on his suspenders before settling his gun belt around his waist. Like all reasonable cavalry officers, he never bothered with the heavy saber except for parades and during inspections. A pistol always proved more effective from horseback than the clumsy sword.

"You don't have to ride out until dawn," Fargo said. "Nothing might happen, if I'm successful. And if I'm not, you'll have your hands full." Fargo thought this arrangement best. If he failed to free the children, Sawyer would hurry them to Benavidez. That meant Captain Chapman had to intercept the gambler and ranchero.

"I can use a few more hours of shut-eye," admitted Chapman. "You riding back out right away?"

"I have to, if I want to get to the camp where the slavers are holding their captives before dawn."

"Are you sure you don't want some men to go with you?"

"I'll be fine," Fargo said. "I won't fail you, Captain."

Chapman sank to his cot and put his face in his hands. Fargo took that as his cue to leave. Outside in the cold night air, he pulled the report from under his shirt and held it up. Chapman's signature at the bottom was plain enough for anyone to read. Fargo folded the paper so that the signature showed and precious little else, then set off for the guardhouse. Desperate times called for desperate measures.

"Halt, who goes there!" came the immediate challenge. Fargo knew Chapman kept his troopers alert with snap inspections, but he had hoped for a little less attention tonight.

"It's me. Fargo."

"How you doin', sir?" asked the sentry. The guard lowered his musket. "Why are you here?"

Fargo took a deep breath, then plunged into his story. "I got orders from Captain Chapman to take charge of the prisoner."

"Broken Finger? The captain wants him released?"

"In my custody. Here's the order. That's Captain Chapman's signature at the bottom." Fargo held out the report he had taken from the captain's office, banking on the fact that the guard could not read. However, the man had seen orders posted over his commander's signature enough times to recognize it.

"This is mighty strange, if you don' mind me sayin' so, sir," the guard said. "I wasn't tole nuthin' about let-tin' that heathen go."

"Here it is. We need to be on our way quick. The whole post is going on maneuvers at dawn."

The guard frowned, then brightened. He waved and called, "Sarge! Sergeant! Come on over. Mr. Fargo's got orders from the captain for you!"

Fargo knew Sergeant Sallin could read and would know this was not an order releasing Broken Finger.

He was caught.

11

"What's your problem, Private?" The sergeant saun-tered over, glanced at Fargo, then faced the guard squarely. "You supposed to be lollygaggin' with the scout?"

"Not like that, Sarge. Honest. He—"

Fargo knew he had to head this off before it snowballed.

"I was responsible, Sergeant," Fargo said. "I was ask-ing the private about the Navajo prisoner I brought in." He saw the guard frown, trying to figure out if this really was what Fargo had been about. "I need to talk to him to see if I can get information from him."

"What information? He's been locked up a couple days. What would that Injun know that he could tell you?" Sergeant Sallin stared curiously at Fargo.

"There's a lot of slavery going on, Sergeant," Fargo said. "Broken Finger knows something about the trade."

"Of course he does. The son of a bitch is responsible for most of it. Him and the rest of those heathen Nava-jos have grabbed more settlers than you can shake a stick at."

"Can I talk to him?"

"Let him go palaver, Private. What's going to happen? He ain't about to let the heathen go, now is he?" The sergeant laughed. Everyone at Fort Fauntleroy had talked in hushed awe about how Fargo had gone into the enemy's stronghold and had returned with Broken Finger. It was the stuff of legends.

Of course he would never think of letting the wily Navajo chief go free.

"Thanks, Sergeant," Fargo said, breathing a sigh of relief. He had dodged a bullet on this one. He watched the sergeant of the guard continue on his rounds, checking other sentries scattered around the compound, and making certain nothing at the perimeter of the low adobe fence required his personal attention.

"Mr. Fargo, I don't unnerstand," the guard said, scratching his head. "You tole me you wanted Broken Finger turned free. But you tole the sergeant that—"

"Don't worry about misunderstanding me," Fargo said. The puzzled guard shrugged it off and led him toward the four cells in the blockhouse they used as a stockade. When they stepped into the room, Broken Finger sat up on the narrow cot. His eyes were pools of glittering dark fire as they fixed on Fargo.

Fargo said nothing until the private left to return to his post. "I think I've found your son," he then said. This brought the Navajo to his feet and over to the bars, his powerful hands trying to bend the iron so he could get free.

"You play with me!" he accused.

"It's true, but he's being held by five or six men. Maybe more. I need help getting him free, him and eighteen others." Fargo did not mention the boy shot down by Sawyer's gang. Not knowing which of the children was Broken Finger's son made him wary to say too much.

"Get the cavalry to attack," Broken Finger said caustically. "That is what they want to do—kill."

"There's not much chance Captain Chapman could sneak up on the gang, not where they have their camp. Someone used to moving quiet has to go in."

"You did not free them?"

"I couldn't," Fargo said honestly. "Two men together could, though. One to distract and the other to get the children away from captivity."

"I will kill the slavers!"

"You'll do as you have to," Fargo said sharply. "See to it that the children get away. You can speak to them, and they'll do as you say." To the Indian youth, one white man was the same as another. But freeing children, including his own—held as slaves, transcended all else.

"Get me out!"

Fargo's lips thinned to a grim line.

"That's going to be something of a problem," he said. "I tried to get you out using a forged order, but it didn't work."

"So Chapman will not release me?" Broken Finger spat. "I thought so. You lie. You all lie!"

"I'll get you out, but we have to do it so no one knows. Chapman will be going out on patrol at dawn, taking most of the soldiers with him. No one's likely to check on you after that. But by then we have to be at Sawyer's camp."

"Sawyer? He is the one who kidnapped my son?"

"You get ready to leave. I'll be back," Fargo promised. He left, nodding in the private's direction. Getting Broken Finger free by subterfuge had not worked, thanks to the sergeant's untimely appearance. He had to do something even more daring if he wanted to free Broken Finger in time to catch Sawyer and his gang at their camp.

Fargo rode into Ojo del Oso, noting that most folks were sound asleep in their beds. The only place in town still showing any life was the saloon. Fargo circled the Silver Centavo, looking for someone he could use as a ruse in his bid to get Broken Finger out of the fort stockade.

Two men inside the saloon drank slowly, nursing their beers. Fargo had seen this before. The men had run out of money but refused to give up and go home. If they even had homes.

As Fargo kept riding, an idea came to him. At the rear of Austin Kincaide's general store he found the man he needed. Sleeping off a drunk caused by too much Taos Lightning, a corporal from the fort lay on the ground outside the store. Chapman might have him thrown into military prison if the corporal missed muster at dawn.

In a way, Fargo thought he was doing the noncom a favor. He wrestled the soldier over the rump of the

Ovaro, then mounted and rode fast, getting back to Fort Fauntleroy. Fargo made a point of avoiding the sergeant on his patrol, determined to deal only with the gullible private on duty in front of the guardhouse.

He dismounted and went to the private.

"What you got there, Mr. Fargo?" the guard asked. "Why, that looks like Anthony. You got Corporal Anthony!"

"Hush," Fargo said. "Not so loud. I'm doing the corporal a favor. He tied one on and is in no condition to be anywhere until he sleeps off the drunk he's been on. Help me get him in the guardhouse."

"You gonna lock him up?"

"It's where he belongs, isn't it?"

"Well, yeah, I reckon," the private said.

"Wait," Fargo said when they got the corporal to the door into the guardhouse. "If the sergeant sees you've left your post, he might come over. You wouldn't want Anthony to get into any more trouble—and you'd be in it with him."

"What are we gonna do?"

Fargo forced himself to keep from smiling.

"Give me the keys and I'll put the corporal into a cell, cover him up and no one will know, except you. Just before you go off duty at dawn, tell your relief the corporal's sentence is up and to let him out."

"All right," the private said dubiously. "I owe the corporal a favor or two. He's always been real good to me."

"The keys," Fargo said, not wanting to give the private the chance to think over his "favor."

He took the ring from the soldier and carried Anthony inside. Broken Finger was on his feet, hands gripping the bars so tightly his knuckles turned white. Fargo tossed the Navajo chief the keys and dragged the corporal to the cell.

"Get him onto your bunk," Fargo said, "and cover him up all the way." It would be impossible for anyone to tell this was not Broken Finger.

"I will kill the guard and—"

"No need. Use some of your skill and get away without anyone seeing you," Fargo snapped. "Fort Fauntleroy is going to be stirring in an hour or so, every soldier ready for action. If they find a dead sentry, all that fire-power will be aimed at you."

"I can defeat them all!"

"And let your son be sold to slaveholders down in Mexico?" Broken Finger's face rippled as his emotions conflicted. He was a warrior, a fighter, a chief who had been disgraced. Killing many of the bluecoats would restore his honor.

And if he did this, he would never see his son again.

"Where can I get a horse?" Broken Finger asked. Fargo grinned, then motioned for the chief to follow him.

While Fargo distracted the private by giving him back the ring of keys, Broken Finger moved from shadow to shadow until he neared the fort corral. The horses began stirring restlessly as the unknown intruder approached them.

"What's that?" asked the private, bringing up his musket.

"I'll go see. Don't worry your head, Private," Fargo said, slapping the soldier on the back. "It's probably a coyote giving the horses fits."

"All right, sir," the private said. "I'd better git on back to my sentry duty."

Fargo hurried to the corral and spent a few minutes calming the horses. He led the gentlest one from the corral, passing the animal over to Broken Finger. The Navajo hastily put on the bridle and looked at Fargo for a moment.

"You will not fail me?"

"We ride out real slow, you following me. Keep low on the horses so it'll look as if I'm leading a riderless horse. Then we'll gallop to Sawyer's camp."

Fargo worried that time worked against him. It was only an hour until dawn. Chapman would be mustering his troops soon. Fargo wanted to rescue the children before the cavalry got into action, even if Chapman headed for Benavidez's hacienda and not Sawyer's camp out on the Santa Fé road.

"You leaving already, Fargo?" called the sergeant.

The noncom sat on the low adobe wall not twenty feet away. Fargo glanced over his shoulder and saw Broken Finger clinging to the side of the horse away from the sergeant. The darkness hid his moccasined foot atop the horse and as well as his arm around its strong neck.

"Got to ride far and hard, Sergeant," Fargo called back. "Be with you after I do some scouting on Benavidez's rancho."

"That where we're heading?" asked Sallin.

Fargo cursed the sergeant's need to talk.

"I'm going to let the captain tell you everything. You might get a jump on him by seeing that your musket's clean and your six-shooter's loaded."

"Thanks, Fargo." The sergeant stood and started for the barracks, never looking back. Fargo urged his Ovaro forward at a trot, wanting to get as far from the fort as he could.

A short way from the entrance to the fort, Fargo turned and called to Broken Finger, "Get on top of your horse. They can't see us anymore."

With a motion like flowing liquid, Broken Finger gained his seat.

"Where do we go?" the Navajo demanded.

"A couple miles that way," Fargo said, pointing in the direction of Santa Fé. He held Broken Finger to a trot, not wanting to exhaust their horses. If things had been different, he would have brought horses for each of the children to help their escape. But he had to work with what resources he had.

"If you can, steal their horses," Fargo said to the intent Broken Finger.

"You are *telling* me to be a horse thief?" Broken Finger laughed. "It is only fair payment for what they have done."

"No," Fargo said, "they need to pay more than losing a horse or two." He would prefer seeing nooses around all of their filthy necks, but that was ultimately up to Captain Chapman.

Bringing everyone involved in the slave trade to justice might just cause a range war. If it did, Fargo wanted the Navajos and other Indians clear of it. The last thing anyone needed was adding more rifles to such a fight. Conflict between *los ricos* and the soldiers from Fort Fauntleroy was bad enough, but such a fight would involve all the settlers, white as well as Mexican.

"Here, into the foothills," Fargo called to Broken Finger. The Navajo was perhaps too intent. For the first time, Fargo realized Broken Finger didn't have any weapons except his own hatred and need for revenge. A knife would be useful, but Fargo was not inclined to offer his Arkansas toothpick to the chief. Not yet. And he wasn't handing over his Henry to anyone.

"The trail," Broken Finger said. "I see it."

Fargo frowned, then reined back and dismounted. How had the Indian seen the trail in the dark? Fargo looked up and saw the first light of a false dawn beginning to glow on the eastern horizon. But it was not enough for Broken Finger to pick up the trail.

Fargo mounted and trotted after Broken Finger, now almost a quarter of a mile up into the hills. The land got rough fast, slowing him. Somehow Broken Finger kept up the pace, even scrambling faster. He was like a racehorse upon seeing the finish line.

Fargo wanted to call out for the Navajo chief to stop so that they could coordinate their attack. While Broken Finger freed the children, Fargo had to engage Sawyer's gang. With any luck, the children would escape—and so would Fargo. Then it would be up to Captain Chapman to round up the slavers.

For the moment, winning had to be rescuing those Sawyer had kidnapped.

"Where, Fargo, where?" demanded Broken Finger, looking around frantically. "I do not see the trail!"

"Be quiet," Fargo cautioned. "We're almost on top of them."

Broken Finger's eyes snapped up as he studied the higher terrain where a sentry might be posted. Fargo had already looked but saw no one guarding the camp. Texas Jack Sawyer was an arrogant son of a bitch and probably thought no one could find him. From all Fargo had seen of the men riding with Sawyer, they wouldn't take kindly to Sawyer ordering them around, either.

That worked in his favor. They wouldn't have guards on their remuda, making it simple for Broken Finger to steal their horses.

"The rope corral is off in that direction. Get the boys first. They had them tied up a hundred yards higher into the hills. I'll stir them up so you can work without getting caught."

"I won't be seen," Broken Finger said hotly.

"Don't do anything stupid," Fargo warned. "We free the children first and then get them away from the gunfighting. Then you can do whatever you want to Sawyer and his gang."

Fargo intended to hightail it unless he could find the opportunity to take out all the owlhoots. Then it would be his pleasure and privilege to remove such scum from New Mexico Territory.

"Here," Fargo said, handing Broken Finger his Colt. "You've only got six shots. Be careful."

"I will be brave!" Broken Finger hesitated a moment, then nodded once in Fargo's direction. Even with his incredible skills, Fargo was hard-pressed to follow Broken Finger's swift movement through the rocks. The man moved like a puff of wind and far quieter. When Broken Finger had disappeared from sight, Fargo hefted his Henry and made sure his toothpick was close at hand.

Then he went off to find Sawyer and raise a little hell.

Only an occasional rock turning under his boots marked his movement. If he had worn moccasins like Broken Finger, Fargo might have moved noiselessly. As it was, he traded speed for sound, picking his way quickly through the rocky terrain. He stopped when smoke from a wood fire made his nostrils twitch.

Getting his bearings, Fargo moved to the draw leading into the sandy area where Sawyer and the others had pitched their camp. Rifle leveled, he advanced. The pungent scent of burning wood and coffee grew stronger, but so did an uneasy feeling deep in his gut.

Rushing forward, Fargo burst into the sandy spit and looked around. A scraping of leather against rock caused him to whirl about, his Henry rifle aimed up to the top of a huge boulder—at Broken Finger.

"They are gone," Broken Finger said angrily.

Fargo lowered his rifle, feeling like he had been cheated.

"Then we'd better get on their trail and run those sons of bitches into the ground," he said, his ire matching the flash in the Navajo chief's eyes.

12

"The corral was up there," Fargo said. "If they all rode out, they'll have left a passel of tracks for us to follow." It bothered Fargo that they had not passed Sawyer and the others on their way to the camp. Not seeing any tracks on the way in meant that Sawyer had hightailed it in some other direction.

Fargo wended his way through the tumble of rocks until he reached the three gnarled cottonwoods that had been used as posts for the rope corral. The ground was cut up, showing Sawyer and his gang had left without trying to be subtle. A blind man could follow this trail.

Fargo shook his head and said, "I don't understand where they are going. Benavidez's hacienda is in the other direction. Do you know what's at the top of this ridge?" Fargo squinted into the new sun poking up over the horizon. Sawyer and his men had taken their captives upslope, not down to the road leading to Benavidez's hacienda.

"Where does any road go?" asked Broken Finger. "Follow it in one direction, and you end up opposite to the other."

"Villanueva's hacienda? Is it in this direction?" Fargo asked, wondering if the other *patrón* might be cutting himself into the deal. He had championed Benavidez and gotten him out of the stockade. There might be a business connection as well as one of comradeship between the men. The settlers seemed to think *los ricos* were all in cahoots in every matter. They might very well be.

"No, it lies alongside Benavidez's hacienda, to the

south," Broken Finger said. "The *malpais* is there. Not up here." The Navajo pointed first in the direction Fargo had thought Sawyer would ride, then uphill to the top of the mountain. If Sawyer got away, he could lose himself in the winding canyons, giving Fargo only a small chance of ever finding him. Rocky trails, and knowledge that the cavalry might be after him would turn Sawyer cagey.

But Fargo also knew the gambler was arrogant to the point of stupidity. Fargo had to count on that or the children would be sent off to Mexico as servants for some rich *patrón*.

"Let's ride," Fargo said, turning back downhill to fetch his horse, and stewing at how everything had gone wrong. Sawyer heading out in this direction told Fargo that the cavalry would be patrolling empty land. Captain Chapman would find nothing illegal on Benavidez's land. Fargo had naïvely assumed that the transfer of gold for slaves would take place at the same location as the meeting between Benavidez and Sawyer. It had not occurred to him that they might have a regular transfer point far removed from the *malpais*.

Broken Finger rode silently at Fargo's side. In the wan light, they followed the trail easily. Sawyer had made no effort to hide where he headed. Once, Fargo jumped down and examined the soft dirt alongside the harder packed trail. A small bare foot had made a print. Sawyer walked his prisoners rather than letting them ride.

Fargo glanced up at Broken Finger. The Navajo chief sat impassively for a moment, then said, "He will kill any of them who slow him."

"He's already shot one trying to escape," Fargo said before he realized it. Broken Finger jerked as if someone had driven a knife deep into his ribs. "I'm sorry. I didn't want to mention it since I don't know who it was that Sawyer's men killed."

Broken Finger said nothing. His jaw set firmly and his dark eyes burned with hatred. He urged his stolen cavalry mount ahead without saying a word. Fargo followed, worrying that the Indian might miss some sign in his anger. He did not know Broken Finger well enough, it seemed. The chief saw evidence the kidnappers had left on the hard, rocky trail before Fargo.

The only bright spot was that Sawyer refused to let his captives ride. That would slow his escape. Less than ten minutes later when this notion came to Fargo, he held up his hand to stop Broken Finger from riding on. Rocks had been dislodged all over the trail, as if the horses had gathered for a few minutes. Fargo cocked his head to one side and listened hard.

Broken Finger nodded. He heard the horses, too. They dismounted, Fargo taking his Henry. He felt a trifle uneasy that Broken Finger still held his Colt, but in a fight they would need all the firepower they could deliver. He wished he trusted the Navajo chief more.

And Fargo knew Broken Finger had no reason at all to trust him.

They slipped forward, cresting the ridge and keeping low to prevent being silhouetted against the rising sun. For a few seconds, they took in the scene in front of them. Without any need for agreement, they split, Broken Finger darting to the left uphill and Fargo circling right to reach a crevice where he could get the drop on Texas Jack Sawyer and the five men with him.

Fifteen shots in the Henry, six men. Fargo considered those odds about even. What tipped the scales in Sawyer's favor were the eighteen young boys all tied together at the neck. It did no good if he brought down Sawyer after the gambler had killed any—or all—of the captives.

"Where is he?" groused one of Sawyer's men.

"He'll be here. You know how them Mexicans are," Sawyer said. "Maybe he ought to buy himself a good watch." As if to make the point, he reached into the pocket on his brocade vest and pulled out a watch, making a big deal out of opening the ornate gold case and studying the dial.

Fargo fumed as he waited for Broken Finger to get into position. His only clue the Navajo was ready came when a shadow moved across the ground near a low-growing, scrubby piñon. Fargo hefted his rifle, took a deep breath, then squeezed off a shot that took the hat off Sawyer's nearest henchman.

The man yelped and dropped to the ground. Fargo fired again, this time trying to take out Sawyer. The gambler's luck held. Fargo missed him and the shot ricocheted away. The confusion in the tight knot of kidnappers and victims mounted.

"There, up in the rocks. A posse!" cried one kidnapper.

"No, you danged fool. There's only one. Get him!" shouted Sawyer. But he made no effort to join the three of his men trying to get Fargo in their sights.

Fargo had enough time to line up another of Sawyer's gang. This time his bullet flew straight and true. The man grunted, bolted up, and then twisted to the ground as if all the bones in his body had turned to water. Fargo kept firing, but he only winged one of the two others.

He started firing as fast as he could lever rounds into the Henry's chamber when he saw Broken Finger make his move. His rapid firing drove the kidnappers to the ground and masked the Navajo's movements. A quick shot in Sawyer's direction caused the gambler to dive for cover, leaving the eighteen boys standing alone, all tied up.

Broken Finger burst from cover and ran over to them. Sawyer saw the Navajo and tried to shoot him, but Broken Finger starting using Fargo's Colt. He fired wildly, six shots ringing out as fast as the Colt could be cocked and triggered.

Fargo was counting; Sawyer was not. The gambler did not realize the Navajo chief was out of ammo when he turned and ran.

Fargo came out of the crevice and tried to get Sawyer in his sights, but the gambler was running too fast. When the men who had come after Fargo saw him shift targets, they opened up on him. Bullets careened off the rocks on either side of him, forcing Fargo back. He missed his shot at Sawyer and had no chance at either of the men trying to ventilate him.

Back-pedaling, Fargo caught his heel and sat down hard. He scrambled to get to his feet but the bullets bouncing from one side of the crevice to the other kept him crowded low. Fargo dug in his heels and pushed himself farther into the crevice, looking for a way out. What had started as a good ambush spot now turned into a death trap.

He had been protected when no one knew where he was. Now all the kidnappers had to do was fire into the narrow crevice and they'd have a good chance of hitting him. Worse, Fargo could no longer hope to wing any of them as long as they didn't show themselves in the narrow opening.

When his shoulders wedged into the narrowing crevice, Fargo knew it was time to get away. He could not retreat further. Glancing up, he saw lightening sky above. He had dropped into the crevice close to the clearing where Sawyer and the others had waited. Now Fargo had to get out of the ragged crevice at its narrowest spot. Forcing his back against one side and getting his knees up, he inched toward the top of the enclosing rocks.

Bullets continued to sing past him, one grazing his cheek and leaving a stinging bloody streak. That they still fired at him heartened him. This meant Broken Finger had that much better of a chance escaping with his son and the others from his tribe.

But if it meant good things for Broken Finger and the kidnapped boys, it turned nastier by the second for Fargo. A second bullet creased his thigh, momentarily weakening him. He slid back a few inches, wedging himself in. Using the butt of his Henry, he levered himself upward and continued his painfully slow climb. Before he reached the top, he awkwardly fired a couple of rounds down the narrow crevice to keep the kidnappers back.

He exploded upward, twisting lithely and flopping down on his belly on top of the rock.

For a brief instant Fargo felt a surge of triumph. He had escaped.

Then he realized how wrong he was.

Fancy hand-tooled boots were level with his gaze. As he looked up, he stared into the barrel of a Remington held by Benavidez. Fargo sensed rather than saw the vaqueros with the ranchero. He had come out of the death trap crevice only to be caught by the very men coming to buy the slaves.

"You are a foolish man, Fargo," Benavidez said coldly. "You have cost me a great deal of money. I do not permit anyone to deprive me of money. In your case, it is worse. You might as well have stolen it from me."

"My apologies," Fargo said sarcastically.

Fargo let a vaquero rip the Henry from his grip. Another pulled him roughly to his feet. Being wedged into the tight crevice had cramped him a little, but he was ready for a fight.

But Benavidez wanted nothing of it. The ranchero stepped up and swung his Remington, the hard barrel crashing into the side of Fargo's head as the vaquero clung to his arm to prevent him from moving. Fargo sagged down, dazed. He felt the world closing in around him, blackness replacing the new dawn. He knew if he gave in now, there might never be another sunrise for him.

He slumped weakly, letting the vaquero support his entire weight.

"He is not so tough." The vaquero holding him laughed.

"Perhaps not," Benavidez said. "Perhaps this has all been a bad dream and he has never existed. Take him down to the meeting spot where Sawyer failed to deliver the slaves."

Fargo was roughly dragged over rocks and thorny shrubs. He made no effort to escape. Not yet. He got his wits back and made certain the vaqueros were overly confident and off guard. He would have one chance to escape and that would be it.

After they pulled him along the soft dirt a few yards more, his toes digging into the ground, Fargo acted. He stiffened his legs and shoved downward as hard as he could. This yanked him away from the lax grips on his arms. He got his hands under him, checked his fall, then rolled to one side, knocking over one man like he was the lone remaining pin in a game of skittles.

As their legs intertwined, Fargo grabbed the pistol from the man's belt and fired before he had it fully free. The bullet ripped into the vaquero's gut. The Mexican screeched in pain and flinched back, giving Fargo the chance to shoot his other captor.

The vaquero was going for his six-shooter but Fargo's bullet ripped through his chest before the man's fingers could curl around the butt of the pistol. The world began to move in a whirl around Fargo. He heard Benavidez yelling, guns firing, horses neighing.

He came to his knees, fired again, and winged another man. Fargo tried to get some idea how many vaqueros he faced. He didn't care how many of Benavidez's men he killed, but the rounds in the stolen six-gun were going to come up empty before he finished shooting them all. He threw himself to the side, hit the ground, and rolled again as bullets sang past his head. He got his feet under him and dug in, running hard for cover.

He almost made it.

A bullet hit the heel of his boot, tripping him. Fargo fell face-forward on the rocky ground and lost his six-shooter as he crashed down. Then it felt as if the heavens above collapsed on him.

The first blow came from Benavidez. The next was delivered by a vaquero at the ranchero's side. That was followed by heavy kicks, with the coup de grâce a heavy rock thrown from high above him. This time he did not need to fake being stunned.

"Enough with this one," snapped Benavidez. "I want him to die slowly. He has killed Gordo and Jaime!"

"He shot me in the arm," whined another.

"He shot *me* in the leg!" complained another. "Look? See how I bleed?"

"No more of this," Benavidez said, motioning impatiently to his surviving vaqueros for silence. "No more of *him*!"

Benavidez went to Fargo's side and kicked him as hard as he could in the ribs, the fancy hand-tooled boot spattering with blood as it tore into Fargo's skin. Fargo was pushed over the edge into complete darkness.

13

Pain. Pain in his back, along his sides, across his chest, but mostly all over his face. Fargo tried to touch his forehead and found he could not. His arms refused to move. He struggled, trying to roll onto his side. When new pain shot up his arms like someone had raked a dull knife along his wrists, Fargo realized, through the haze of confusion, that he was staked out spread-eagle.

He opened his eyes and immediately shut them again. He was tied to the ground so that he faced straight into the sun. Turning his head to one side allowed him to open his eyes cautiously and look around. All he saw at first was the heavy stake driven into the ground and the cruel rawhide strip tied around his left wrist. Turning in the other direction showed him what he had already figured out. His right hand was similarly tied down.

"You will die," came a mocking voice. "I dismissed my vaqueros so I could savor your death all by myself. Besides, I did not want you to die with *too* many people about. I prefer to be the last one you see before you go to your richly deserved hell."

"Benavidez," Fargo said through cracked lips. His tongue felt as if it had grown to twice its normal size and someone had filled the rest of his mouth with cotton. "Why should I bother to go to hell when I have the devil here with me?"

Benavidez laughed harshly. Boots grated on the loose gravel and for a brief instant Fargo felt intense relief as Benavidez's body blocked out the burning sun. He looked up at the ranchero and saw more than cruelty in his face. He saw his own death. Fargo had always known the life he led was dangerous and that he could die at any time. He had always thought it would be a hungry grizzly that mauled him, or a bullet that robbed him of life.

What rankled him more than the notion that this was the day he would die was that Benavidez would get so much pleasure from it.

"I will make you wish you had never come to New Mexico Territory," Benavidez promised. "It is my task, however, to divert you from thinking this until a few seconds before you die. That way you can concentrate on suffering before that final wish."

"Are you going to talk me to death?"

Anger flashed across Benavidez's swarthy face, then the ranchero calmed.

"You are a different breed of man. Those Americans I know are weak and seek only money. They would sell each other into slavery if I offered enough. But you are not like them. Seeing you die slowly will be a great pleasure."

Benavidez bent over. Fargo was momentarily blinded as sunlight again burned his eyes. He felt something warm and oozing dribble into his bare chest and then run down his sides. Sniffing, he recognized what Benavidez poured all over him.

Honey.

This would draw desert ants to gnaw at his flesh. One or two ant bites were tolerable. Fargo had endured far worse. But a dozen? A hundred? Ten thousand? The agony would be accelerated by the sun blistering his flesh, hour after hour. The brutally hot New Mexico summer sun could kill any exposed man, no matter how strong.

Debilitated by the ant bites, Fargo would die before sundown.

If Fargo was lucky, he would die before the scavengers came out to feed on his almost-dead carcass. As if this thought was obvious, Benavidez laughed heartily.

"You understand, I see. Good. Would not a drop of water on your lips be welcome?" Fargo turned his head slightly and saw Benavidez pouring water from a canteen onto the thirsty sand. He tried to hold back but could not restrain himself. He surged, trying to get just a drop on his parched lips.

This brought forth new laughter from the ranchero.

"You are not so tough, are you? You are like all the others. The difference is that you have cost me much money. I should tend to my rancho, see to making more money, but instead I will take this day until your bones are picked clean by insects. Have any begun dining on your putrid flesh yet?"

Even as Benavidez taunted him, Fargo winced. A sharp, tiny sting told him the first of the ants had arrived. He closed his eyes and tried to calm himself. If he panicked, he could never escape. How he might get free was beyond Fargo at the moment, but he focused his hatred on Benavidez and what he would do to the ranchero after he got free.

Two more sharp, quick stings. Then another, and another. The feasting had begun.

Noon. The sun beat down on his blistered face. Fargo had thought the wind and weather had turned his skin to leather capable of withstanding even the noonday sun. He was wrong.

The agony from the insect bites continued to keep him from passing out. He experienced such weakness in his arms and legs that he could hardly stir now, even when new ants bit at his body.

And above it all, through a red haze of pain, drifted Benavidez. The man no longer taunted him with the promise of water but openly drank to make the torture that much worse. It seemed that the more Fargo suffered, the more Benavidez enjoyed it. Fargo constantly tensed and relaxed his right arm, trying to work loose the stake in the ground.

Was there a little movement? Did he pull the stake free enough so that he could swing the sharp wooden spike around like a flail, and perhaps drive it into Benavidez's foul heart?

The stake remained secure in the ground.

Fargo passed out. Again.

*   *   *

"Why won't you die so I can return to my hacienda?"

The question echoed down from the tops of the four Navajo holy mountains, from Mount Taylor and San Francisco Peak and Big Sheep Mountain and Sierra Blanca. It was distant and cold and somehow special for Skye Fargo. It took him seconds to realize why.

He was irritating Benavidez. He had not died like the ranchero had thought.

Squinting, Fargo peered up and saw Benavidez standing by him. The expression on the man's face sent a surge of strength through Fargo's veins. He had not begged. This only goaded Benavidez to his tortures. But Fargo had not died, either, and this angered the ranchero. Anything he could do to make Benavidez mad added to his own strength.

"I haven't killed you yet," Fargo rasped out. "Can't die until I do. Then I'll die happy."

"You'll die in misery!" raged Benavidez. He kicked Fargo, but the pain was a distant echo of what he had suffered already.

His mind began to drift as the pain subsided. Again his thoughts turned to the Navajo holy mountains. He had never learned their Navajo names, only which of those in the surrounding mountains were considered holy by the Navajos. This point bothered Fargo, and he could not figure out why.

Why care what the Navajos called their holy places?

Why think of the Navajos at all?

Fargo was not certain what drew his attention away from Benavidez to the rocks beyond. He had been brought to a mesa with a clear view of the surrounding countryside. There might be some special reason Benavidez wanted him to die here, or perhaps it was simply convenient. If Fargo had been able to study the surrounding terrain he might have discovered others brought to their deaths by Benavidez's cruel torture.

Now, he was less interested in the ranchero than he was in the dark shape flowing over the edge of the mesa and coming toward them.

"Who's that?" he got out, not thinking straight. Fargo

had always wondered what Death looked like. He was going to find out, as Death came right for him.

Benavidez stared, then grabbed for his six-shooter and drew it. The Remington belched white smoke three times.

"Navajos!" Benavidez backed away, holding his six-gun out, elbow locked and sighting along the entire length of the weapon. He fired again. This produced a shrill, girlish cry.

Fargo forced himself to lift his head and see who Benavidez shot at. His target was an Indian boy, perhaps ten or eleven. Fargo tried to remember where he had seen the boy before. Then he heard the slicing sound of a knife and his right arm jerked free. The sudden pain of the circulation returning to his wrist made him cry out.

A second cut severed the rawhide on his left wrist. He looked around and saw Broken Finger flip his knife around as he stalked Benavidez.

Fargo might have inadvertently cried out or Benavidez might have been keyed up and alert to any small noise. Something gave Broken Finger away before he could lift his knife and bring it slashing down across Benavidez's back.

The ranchero darted to one side, and Broken Finger narrowly missed with a killing stroke. Benavidez fired, filling the air with choking white gunsmoke. Fargo found himself sitting up and wrenching free the stakes at his ankles so that he could join the fight. He wanted Benavidez for his own. After all he had endured, Broken Finger owed him the privilege of this kill.

Benavidez fired again. The round caught Fargo in the shoulder as he staggered forward. He spun about and crashed into Broken Finger, and the two of them tumbled to the ground. The Navajo chief pushed Fargo aside roughly, struggling to get back to his feet.

"Wait!" Broken Finger cried out as the boy rushed past them, brandishing a knife of his own. But the boy paid no attention, intent on gutting Benavidez.

The ranchero fired point blank. Fargo expected a loud report and the boy to die on the spot. Instead, the Remington coughed asthmatically and spewed out a burning wad along with a poorly propelled slug. The boy's shirt singed and the bullet did not stop him.

Knife high, the boy tried to kill Benavidez. The ranchero swung the long-barreled six-gun and caught the boy on the side of the head, knocking him to the ground. As Broken Finger fought to get to his feet, Benavidez turned and ran like a deer.

"Die!" shrieked Broken Finger, finally getting to his feet and taking off after the frightened man. The Navajo stumbled and fell over the boy, came to one knee, then stopped his pursuit to see if the youth was all right.

Fargo painfully stumbled over to them. Seeing the two together, he knew this was Broken Finger's son. Somewhere in the back of his head he came up with the name.

"Are you hurt, Shaking Leaf?"

Both Broken Finger and the boy turned dark eyes on him. The boy's chin set, and he thrust out his thin chest.

"I am Navajo," he said.

"Go after Benavidez," Fargo said, seeing the boy was unharmed. The burning wad had singed his hide shirt and the bullet had left a blood blister on Shaking Leaf's shoulder. Otherwise, the only affliction the boy suffered from was hatred.

Fargo found that he shared this. If he had been able, he would have gone after Benavidez and strangled him with his bare hands. As it was, he sank down beside Shaking Leaf. The boy looked him over and sneered, as if saying Fargo's painful injuries were nothing to a Navajo warrior.

Broken Finger jumped to his feet and raced after Benavidez. Before he reached the edge of the mesa, shots rang out. The Navajo chief began dodging. Fargo cursed under his breath. Benavidez had reached his horse and had drawn a rifle.

"Let's go to cover," he said to Shaking Leaf. He reached out to take the boy's arm but was rebuffed.

"If you won't let me help you, then you help me," Fargo said. "I'm not too steady on my feet."

Shaking Leaf approached, hesitant. Then he put a thin arm around Fargo's waist and helped him get out of the sun and away from Benavidez's line of fire. Gratefully,

Fargo sank to the ground. To be in the shade, out of the punishing sun, was a start. He carefully wiped dirt all over his honey-caked flanks, then scraped this muddy mixture off the best he could.

The boy whipped around, knifepoint aimed up for a gutting stroke. Then he relaxed when he saw his father returning. From the look on Broken Finger's face, Fargo knew what had happened.

"He got away," Broken Finger said. "He rode off after killing our horses. We are afoot, and he goes for his vaqueros."

"How far are we from his hacienda?" asked Fargo.

"He can return with a dozen men within the hour," Broken Finger said.

"Then let's not sit around jawing," said Fargo. Using the rocks and Shaking Leaf for support, he got to his feet. Father and son stared at him.

"I don't reckon any lovely young lady's going to ask me to the barn dance with me looking like this, but I'm not *that* ugly."

"You are not able to keep up," Shaking Leaf said. "You will die."

"That's what Benavidez thought, too. I proved him wrong. I'll prove you wrong, too. Where do we go? You know the lay of the land better than I do, and there's not enough time for me to do any scouting."

"You will have to walk on your own," Broken Finger said.

"I'm not asking for anyone's help."

"You are not Navajo," Shaking Leaf said accusingly.

"Quiet," snapped Broken Finger, cutting off his son's bravado. He gestured impatiently, then set off at a brisk walk for the far edge of the mesa. He did not look back to see if Fargo kept up, but Shaking Leaf did several times. The boy's amazement grew as Fargo started out on feeble legs, then gathered strength as he walked.

Fargo stopped and knelt once to pick up his shirt. It was painful to put on over his injuries, but it would be even more painful not to cover the blistered flesh. And the sun was sinking in the west. Soon enough, it would turn downright frigid out on the desert. He would need the shirt to keep warm.

Fargo had to lengthen his stride to make up the distance betwen him the Navajos. They had stopped at the edge of the mesa. For the first time Fargo saw where Benavidez had brought him.

Stretching out as far as the eye could see was the jagged black lava flow of the *malpais.*

If he wanted to stay alive, he had to survive in the worst land New Mexico Territory had to offer—and do it on foot, without weapons or water or food.

"Let's not stand around," he said. "The sooner we get across that patch of land, the sooner we can see to bringing Benavidez to justice."

Both father and son stared at him. The boy didn't know what to make of the comment but Broken Finger clapped Fargo gently on the back and said, "Spoken like a true Navajo." Fargo did not even wince at the sudden pain that touch gave him. The compliment was more than enough to fill him with determination at the honor being bestowed upon him by a Navajo chieftain.

They started down the winding trail that led into the deadly piece of hell.

14

The night chilled Fargo to the bone. He burrowed down in a hollow of black rock and pulled up some vegetation to try to hold in his body heat. How it could be so searing hot during the day and turn so cold at night still amazed him. But it was a fact he had to deal with.

His wounds itched and throbbed, but he had taken care of most of them during the few hours before the sun had set. Prickly pear cactus, growing tenaciously from tight crevices in the lava rock, had given him thick, sticky juices that took away some of the sting from the ant bites. The cuts had been treated with other juices from sere plants found by Broken Finger and Shaking Leaf.

Fargo drifted off to a half-sleep thinking of the boy and his father. They had silently offered him the medicinal plants and had shared what moisture they could from the cacti they found. Their evening meal had been many of the voracious bugs that had already dined on Fargo's flesh. Hunting had been out of the question. They had to keep moving fast to avoid Benavidez's vaqueros.

He did not doubt the ranchero would have his men out scouring the deadly land for them—or their bodies. Benavidez could not afford to let Fargo get away after trying to torture him to death. It was not so much that Fargo was a scout for the cavalry, it had more to do with pride—and fear of reprisal. A man like Skye Fargo would never rest until he had exacted revenge for such abuse.

For Fargo's part, it went further than getting revenge for the brutal torture. Benavidez was a linchpin for the slave trade in this part of New Mexico Territory. Removing him would not make the slave trade dry up, but it would go a ways toward exposing it.

Fargo rubbed his blurred eyes and watched the diamond-hard points of stars in the sky for a while, getting lost in their chilly vastness. A shooting star streaked across the sky, leaving behind a burning trail. Fargo watched until it vanished completely, then slipped into a troubled sleep.

He came awake fast when he felt a hand on his shoulder. Fargo relaxed when he saw Broken Finger crouching by him.

"We must go. There is no time to waste."

Fargo tried to guess the time. It was past midnight from what he could tell by the stars.

"You're right," he said, forcing himself out of the tight notch of rock. He was filthy and ached and needed a few days of sleep, but he'd never get a hot bath and time in bed if Benavidez and his vaqueros caught them.

"Shaking Leaf has spied on *los ricos*. A band comes for us. Twenty or more men."

"Is Benavidez with them?" Fargo asked. If they could hide from or outpace the vaqueros, all that remained was setting up an ambush. Fargo might not die happy if he took Benavidez with him, but he would be a good deal less unhappy seeing the ranchero off to hell first.

"Perhaps. It does not matter. We must go now." Broken Finger tilted his head, indicating the direction they should take. Fargo did not dispute letting Broken Finger decide their course through the *malpais*. This might not be the Navajo's homeland but it was close enough, and Broken Finger had survived countless raids throughout the region.

This time they set off at a deliberate pace, being careful about leaving tracks. Walking on rocks, jumping from one patch of sunbaked ground to another, being sure to erase any footprints made on softer dirt or in sand, they steadily made their way deeper into the middle of the lava rock badlands of the *malpais*.

A half hour of travel helped Fargo fall into a pattern and regain some of his strength and confidence. He kept up with Broken Finger and his son without slowing them down. Their careful travel helped. If the Navajos had declared it was time to break into a ground-devouring trot, Fargo might not have kept up.

He noticed Shaking Leaf slipping away and vanishing through the shadows, heading off at an angle to their travel. Stopping, Fargo cocked his head to one side and heard what the boy already had. Ahead of them, horses nickered. A few seconds after identifying this sound, he heard a man curse in Spanish, followed by a sharp command to be quiet.

Broken Finger held up his hand, indicating they should find a hiding place. Fargo melted into the darkness and waited. Within five minutes, Shaking Leaf returned, passing not ten feet from Fargo's hiding place. From the way the boy moved, Fargo doubted Shaking Leaf knew where he was hiding.

The boy and his father spoke in low tones. It did Fargo no good trying to overhear. They spoke in their special warrior tongue. That the boy knew this language told Fargo how highly Broken Finger thought of him. Only blooded warriors were permitted to use it.

"Well?" Fargo asked. Shaking Leaf jumped, not having located him. Broken Finger's nerves were steadier. He went to Fargo's side and hunkered down.

"Eight vaqueros. All armed. They are resting."

"Can we get their horses?" Fargo asked. This produced a hushed laugh of appreciation from Broken Finger.

"This is the same question my son aksed. Eight armed vaqueros against three with only knives?" Broken Finger shrugged. Then he grinned broadly, his white teeth catching starlight and sparkling. "Why not?"

"Two with knives," Fargo pointed out. Benavidez had taken his Arkansas toothpick, as well as his Henry.

Broken Finger shrugged again, then gestured that they should get to work attacking the vaqueros. Fargo followed, making no more noise than the wind gently caressing the desert sand. He was aware of Shaking Leaf trailing him, but otherwise they might have been alone in the night. This changed fast when he heard sounds ahead.

Broken Finger went left and Shaking Leaf went right, leaving Fargo to find a target in the middle. He carefully advanced, staying low to keep from blocking out the bright stars and revealing his position. The lack of moon helped. He found himself not five feet away from two burly vaqueros. They passed a small glass bottle back and forth. The pungent odor told Fargo they had been patronizing Austin Kincaide's store, buying his illegal Taos Lightning.

The men were not drunk, but their senses were dulled. Fargo did not hesitate. Broken Finger and Shaking Leaf could take care of themselves. With two quick steps, he reached the men. One looked up and choked on the potent liquor. Fargo swung hard and buried his fist in the man's throat. Choking as much from the liquor as the vicious punch, the vaquero fell back. He gagged on his own juices.

The sudden attack caused the other vaquero to stare wide-eyed at his fallen friend. Fargo's brawny arm slipped around the man's throat. A hand on the back of the vaquero's head forced his chin down over a tensed forearm. The vaquero struggled but with his air cut off, those flailings died down quickly as life fled the man's body.

Fargo cast the limp body aside, then drew a knife from the man's belt. He searched for a six-shooter, but the man had ridden off without one. This did not surprise Fargo unduly. Many of the vaqueros were not rich enough to buy a pistol and, for the most part, did not need it while riding the range herding cattle. There would be a rifle with the man's gear, but no six-gun.

Going back to the first man, who still kicked feebly as he drowned in his own blood, Fargo knelt and plucked a six-gun from the man's holster. A quick thrust of the stolen knife put the man out of his misery.

Fargo had killed two of the eight vaqueros without alerting the others. It was time to see to the horses.

He moved silently to his left, looking for Shaking Leaf. He had to step over one vaquero's corpse. The man's throat had been slit. Fargo heard a gasp of pain and moved fast to see what the trouble might be. Shaking Leaf had taken out one of Benavidez's men, but his attack on a second had been less successful.

The vaquero had a knife to the boy's throat. From the set of the man's jaw, he intended to kill Shaking Leaf. Fargo never hesitated. His hand flashed to the six-gun he had shoved into his belt, drew, cocked, and fired before he realized he was acting. The bullet caught the vaquero high on the forehead, snapping his head back.

The instant his grip weakened, Shaking Leaf twisted free, ducked, and spun, his own knife slicing into the man's belly. Fargo was not sure if it was his bullet to the head or Shaking Leaf's knife that had ended the man's life. He was willing to let the boy take credit for the kill, if it enhanced his position among the Navajo warriors. He had to have lost much honor by being taken prisoner by Benavidez's slavers. This might not completely restore him to harmony, but it could not hurt.

Shaking Leaf stared at Fargo, his expression unfathomable.

"The shot alerted them," was all Shaking Leaf said. Then the boy rushed off to find the others.

Fargo heard the thunder of hooves leaving the temporary camp. He found Broken Finger standing over a vaquero, a dripping knife in his hand.

"How many got away?" asked Fargo.

"Three."

"What of the dead ones' horses?" asked Shaking Leaf. "I killed two. I claim their horses as my own!"

Broken Finger and Shaking Leaf both stared at Fargo, as if thinking he would challenge the claim. Fargo was not going to do any such thing. All he wanted was to get back to Fort Fauntleroy now and let Captain Chapman know what was happening. One horse would do him.

"He can have the mount from one of the men I killed, too," Fargo said.

"I do not need gifts!" raged Shaking Leaf.

"Then I give it to you, Broken Finger," Fargo said. "To thank you for saving my life."

Contempt was replaced by an impassive mask on the Navajo chief's face.

"Get the horses. We must ride. Those who escaped will find others to come for us."

Fargo agreed. They spent ten mintes rounding up the scattered horses. Shaking Leaf had three fine horses, Broken Finger a strong mare, and Fargo a steady gelding. As important to him as the horse was the rifle riding in a scabbard at his right knee. He took the canteen and drank deeply. The tepid water refreshed him. The only food in the saddlebags—a bag of beans, flour, bacon—had to be cooked. There was not time.

He drank deeply of the water again, draining the canteen.

"Here," Shaking Leaf said, handing him another canteen. The boy stared at him solemnly.

"Thanks," he said, accepting it. He drank his fill and felt like he could whip his weight in wildcats.

"With horses we can directly cross the *malpais* in two days and avoid Benavidez's vaqueros," Broken Finger said. "They will not come after us. And they will never follow us into Canyon de Chelly." Broken Finger eyed Fargo hotly, daring him to contradict this. Fargo realized the Navajo chief still fumed at being kidnapped from the center of his stronghold. What Broken Finger really meant was apparent.

He did not want Fargo accompanying him back to Dinetah.

That suited Fargo. With a sturdy horse under him, he could get away from Benavidez and report to Chapman on all that had happened. Not only would Benavidez take a fall, so would Texas Jack Sawyer. What this might do to Luella Kincaide he did not know—or care.

Her husband-to-be was a slaver. Her father sold liquor illegally.

Fargo worried more about how all this would affect Dorothea.

"I'll head on back to Ojo del Oso," Fargo said. "By splitting up, we might confuse them and throw them off our trail."

"They will never find *our* trail," boasted Shaking Leaf.

"Then I'll make sure I leave one broad enough to get them coming after me as a diversion. That will let you return to Canyon de Chelly unhindered."

Shaking Leaf bristled. His father put a hand on the boy's shoulder to silence him.

"There is no need. Make all haste to safety, and may they all die painfully!" Broken Finger slashed his knife in the air, then sheathed it. His dark eyes met Fargo's lake blue ones. A momentary flash of friendship passed between them, then vanished.

Without another word, the chief and his son turned their horses into the *malpais* and vanished into the cold night. Fargo remained behind a few minutes, walking from one corpse to the next. He felt like a grave robber, but Benavidez owed him. Stripping the bodies of anything he might use, he stared at a pile of goods. A serape went around his shoulders and chased away some of the chilly night. He placed a few more essential items into the saddlebags on his horse.

Fargo sighed. He intended to get his Ovaro back from Benavidez, but until then this was a good enough mount. Fargo climbed onto the horse, oriented himself by the stars, and headed in an easterly direction, angling away from where he thought the main body of Benavidez's vaqueros might be hunting.

By dawn he reached the edge of the *malpais*, twice going to ground to avoid Benavidez's searching vaqueros. By the following sundown he reached the gates of Fort Fauntleroy.

Tired, hungry even after eating all the food in the saddlebags, he wanted nothing more than to report to Chapman, get the U.S. Army out into the field after Benavidez and Sawyer, then get cleaned up and devour every speck of food he could find in the fort.

Fargo rode slowly to the twin wooden posts marking the entry point to the fort. From both sides came army sentries, their muskets held so tightly the men trembled. Fargo wondered what had the soldiers so stirred up.

"Is the captain in?" he asked a corporal hurrying up to greet him.

"Reckon so, Mr. Fargo." The coldness of the corporal's tone alerted Fargo that something was wrong.

He looked around but saw nothing unusual. If the Navajos had attacked, there would have been guards posted everywhere. As far as he could tell, only the regular number of sentries were on duty. What made him edgy was the way the soldiers seemed to be pointing their muskets in his direction, as if deciding whether to fire or let him ride on.

"What's wrong here, Corporal?"

"Nothing," the noncom said too quickly. "I'll escort you to the captain's office."

Fargo figured the best way of finding out what was wrong was to hear it from the horse's mouth. If Captain Chapman could not tell him, no one at Fort Fauntleroy could.

He dismounted and swung the reins around a hitching post. Fargo noticed how he had drawn quite a crowd, bringing men out of the mess hall to watch. He climbed the three steps to the boardwalk under the broad overhang in front of the captain's office and rapped on the door.

"Come!" barked Chapman. Fargo went in. The fort commander's desk was covered with paperwork. The man struggled to move sheets from one big pile to a smaller one, reading and signing and sometimes crumpling the sheet and tossing it aside. For a moment, Fargo wondered if he had to clear his throat in order to get the officer's attention. What he had to say was important.

When Chapman looked up, he jerked as if someone had stuck him with a pin.

"Fargo!"

"None other than, Captain," Fargo allowed. "I've got a lot of information to give. Most of it's about slave trading. I—"

"I advise you to be quiet until you can engage an attorney."

"What?"

"Sergeant Sallin!" bellowed the captain. The sergeant of the guard must have been hovering outside the door because he came in fast, his hand resting on the holstered pistol at his side.

"Yes, sir?"

"Place Mr. Fargo under arrest and put him in the stockade."

"Wait a minute, Captain. You haven't heard what I have to say! I have proof that Benavidez—"

"Don't say anything, Fargo," cautioned the sergeant. "The captain's in no mood to listen to you, not after you upped and let that savage go free."

Fargo heaved a deep sigh. Chapman had figured out how Broken Finger had escaped. He should have known the officer would be angry about that, especially after specifically denying Fargo permission to let the Navajo chief go. But there was so much Chapman needed to know!

"I can explain all of it. Broken Finger's son was being held by Benavidez and—"

"You can explain it before the judge," Chapman said stiffly. "I put my trust in you, Fargo, and you turned on me. You freed a Navajo responsible for more deaths in New Mexico Territory than I can count. It made me look like a complete fool with Colonel Arnold when he came to see the prisoner."

Fargo tried to keep from smiling. It had to be a jolt expecting to see an infamous Navajo chief in the cell and finding a drunken corporal instead. Any amusement he might have gotten from what had happened quickly evaporated.

"Sergeant, get him to a cell. We will try him as soon as I can get the colonel back from Fort Union!"

"Captain, I had to get Broken Finger out. He—"

Fargo bit off the rest of his explanation. Captain Chapman was not going to listen to him and the sergeant had a pistol shoved painfully into his back. He was led from the commander's office and taken directly to the stockade.

The clanging of the iron-barred door trapping him in the cell sounded like a death knell to Fargo.

It was also a death knell for hundreds of Indian boys and girls who would be spirited off by Benavidez and Sawyer to a life in captivity.

15

"Chain him over there," the sergeant said with some distance. He glared up at Fargo all alone in his cell. The other three cells had been crammed to the point that the soldiers in them sat shoulder-to-shoulder. So many were waiting for summary punishment that the sergeant had to chain other drunkards outside the cells.

"You can always put him in with me," Fargo offered. He chafed at being in the cell for two entire days, with Sawyer and Benavidez continuing their slaving ways outside unchecked, but he had to see some humor in this situation. He was the only prisoner destined for court. As such, the captain had ordered him locked up by himself. This had been before the weekend and a veritable torrent of drunks.

Fargo knew how it went. Right now the Navajo raids were probably at a low. The men were not going after Benavidez because Fargo had not been able to convince their commander of the problem. And doing nothing but boring garrison duty wore on them. Austin Kincaide and his Taos Lightning was the perfect combination to get through some of the monotony.

Friday night had come and most of the soldiers going into Ojo del Oso had ended up staggering drunk. Those granted leave on Saturday night had ended up in the same sorry condition.

"You got more in than out, Sergeant," Fargo pointed out.

"Shut up. The captain wants you kept apart from the others so they don't spoil. Rotten apple in the barrel and all."

"Spoil? Them? They're already pickled," Fargo said.

"We got more men walking punishment duty than we got soldiers to watch over them," Sergeant Sallin complained.

"I know the source of the firewater," Fargo said. "Right now, you've got drunk soldiers to cope with. When the Indians get a barrel or two of that Taos Lightning, they'll really start raising a ruckus. Can you handle it with so many of your men hung over?"

"Who's responsible? Tell me, damn your eyes!" The sergeant growled deep in his throat like an attacking dog. Fargo stood his ground as Sallin grabbed the iron bars and rattled them, as if he were inside glaring out at Fargo.

"That might come up in my court-martial," Fargo said. "Then again, it might not since all I want to do is see an end to the slave trade."

"There's been no more women or children taken in the past week or so," Sergeant Sallin said. "We broke the back of the trade when we raided Benavidez's hacienda and put the fear in him."

"He only sells the slaves. He might not be responsible for capturing them. Someone else is."

"So you say." The sergeant seethed. His jowls quivered and his eyes narrowed to slits. "You really know who's selling the firewater?"

"You want to buy some for your own thirst, Sergeant?" taunted Fargo. He knew he had to make the officer mad or he would never get out of the cell.

"I'll cut your foul tongue out, that's what I want!"

"Sergeant Sallin, as you were," came the hot command. Captain Chapman marched in and stood just beyond arm's reach from the cell.

"Sir, he was tauntin' me and—"

"See to the punishment duty on the parade ground. I think Corporal Ruiz is having problems keeping so many men marching in rank. Private Anthony is giving him special woe."

The sergeant left, shooting Fargo a black look as he exited.

"That means you busted Corporal Anthony in rank,"

Fargo said, savoring the feeling of power he acquired by stating the obvious.

"Is it true, Fargo? You do know who is supplying the liquor to my men?"

"I'm not inclined to lie, Captain." Fargo locked eyes with Chapman, who was tossed on the horns of a real dilemma. His best scout was in the stockade and morale at his post was falling apart before his eyes. Fargo knew how hard it was to stop soldiers from drinking once they got the thirst and found a source. It had ruined more than one command, and was tearing this one apart now.

"But you did let Broken Finger go free."

Fargo said nothing. Any argument on this point had to be made at a court-martial.

"Do you know who is selling the liquor? I've ordered my men not to drink while on furlough, I've made sure they aren't getting any hard liquor at the Silver Centavo, I've restricted them to the fort when they found whiskey elsewhere, I've done everything but assign one man to spy on another, and still I cannot stop the flood of illegal liquor! They are showing up drunk on duty now, and *that* I will not tolerate!"

Fargo knew uttering a single name could put an end to the drunken disobedience at Fort Fauntleroy. The post sutler was responsible for smuggling in and selling the liquor. Chapman had to know Austin Kincaide was responsible, but for some reason he either had not, or could not accuse the storekeeper.

"Do you have any notion who is responsible?"

"I cannot get evidence. How is it you know, Fargo?"

"I'm a good scout. I keep my eyes open."

"That was a slick trick you pulled, substituting a drunken soldier for Broken Finger," Chapman grudgingly admitted. "Finding the man drunk. Is that how you know the responsible party?"

"Can't say it is. I've got my sights set on other targets."

"Then you'll remain in the lockup," Chapman said forcefully. "I will not listen to any further mention about the slave trade since I have decisively ended it."

"Driven the men responsible into hiding—and only

for a while," Fargo said. "What have you heard from the Pueblos and the Navajos on more raids taking their women and children?"

"They are not under my jurisdiction. No whites or Mexicans have been kidnapped. That means the trading is at an end."

"What do you say to this, Captain? If I stop the flood of Taos Lightning into your post, you listen to what I have to say about the slavers?"

"I fear the torrent of liquor will become more serious. If the Indians begin imbibing because I have prevented my soldiers from buying the illegal liquor, that might inflame the entire region."

"You are supposed to keep the peace," Fargo said. "That means keeping the peace between the Indians as well as among the Indians, *los ricos,* and all the other settlers."

"You seem a man of your word, Fargo, although you did release a Navajo warrior." Chapman chewed on his lip. "If you give me your word of honor that you will do what you can to stop the sale of liquor and will not try to escape the charges against you by fleeing, I will let you out."

"You've got yourself some prime jail cell territory to fill, Captain," Fargo said, thrusting his hand through the bars. Chapman hesitated, then shook to seal the deal. It took five minutes to get the sergeant back with the keys to free Fargo.

He stepped out into the blazing sun and saw rank upon rank of soldiers marching punishment duty, muskets on their shoulders, until they wobbled. It would not take much, he thought, to end the trade in Taos Lightning. Once he had the captain back on his side, it wouldn't take much more to stop the slave trade.

"There you are!" Dorothea Kincaide cried. She rushed into Fargo's arms, hers encircling his neck and forcing his head down so that she could plant a big, wet juicy kiss on his lips. "Why haven't you come by? I've missed you, Skye." Dorothea batted her eyelashes and tried to look coy.

"I've been on the trail a long time," he said, not bothering her with the tale of how he had landed in Fort Fauntleroy's stockade.

"And I bet I know how that makes you feel. I feel the same way." She looked around, grabbed Fargo's hand, and pulled him behind her as though she were guiding a small child.

The store was empty because it was the heat of the day. Anyone with any sense had found a cool, shady spot to take a siesta.

"You all alone here?" he asked. "Where's your father?"

"Papa is home resting. Ever since his injuries, he has not felt too well. But I feel fine. And I can see you do, too." She spun about and pressed her ample chest against his. Fargo felt the woman's body responding, hard caps cresting each of her pillowy breasts. Her thin blouse plastered to her body with sweat, giving him a good view of all that the lovely blonde offered.

She wore only a thin undergarment beneath her blouse, and it was drenched with sweat, also. The flare of her breasts made his pulse pound just a little faster. He forgot the reason he had come. Seeing Dorothea drove away all thought of illegal booze and how that whiskey jeopardized peace in New Mexico Territory.

Truth was, Fargo forgot about almost everything when Dorothea reached up and unfastened her blouse, one button at a time. Then she silently peeled away the damp cloth from her smooth white flesh. Fargo reached out and finished the chore for her, slowly revealing the swell of her breasts, then the coppery tips. He bent and swiped his tongue quickly across one nipple and then the other.

Dorothea shuddered and went weak in the knees. She took a step back and braced herself against the counter.

"That feels so nice, Skye. I had almost forgotten what it was like having your mouth moving all over my body."

"You taste . . . salty," he said, licking back and forth between her ample mountains of creamy flesh. His tongue whirled around one taut tip, then slid down into the deep valley between. Back and forth his rough

127

tongue licked before spiraling around and around to the summit of the other breast.

The blonde's body trembled like a leaf in a high wind as he continued mouthing her. His hands moved around and cupped her firm buttocks. Lifting, he got her onto the counter, her sleek legs on either side of his body.

Dorothea threw her arms around his neck again and pulled his face to hers. She kissed him hungrily, as if he were a banquet and she was starving to death. Her fingers ripped at his shirt and fumbled at his gun belt, letting it clatter loudly to the floor. As she pushed his shirt away from his body, she recoiled.

"Skye! What happened to you? You—you're—"

"Yes, I am," he said, too aroused to stop and explain. He kissed her swanlike throat and worked his way up to a tender earlobe. Sucking it between his lips, he teased it with both tongue and teeth. Dorothea gasped and arched her back, thrusting herself forward. Fargo did not stop with his oral assault on her earlobe, teasing and nipping at it until she convulsed in anticipation.

He ran his hands down over her bare flanks, then gathered double handfuls of skirt and tugged insistently. Dorothea knew what he wanted—and it was the same thing she wanted. Her rump lifted off the counter so he could push the useless garment out of the way and expose the paradise nestled between her milky white thighs.

"Damp," he said, running his hand over her nether lips. "Are you sweating?"

"Drooling, my love, drooling!" cried Dorothea. "Now don't torment me anymore. I want you to—oh!" She gasped as his finger intruded in her soft, tender recess. He began whirling it about, stimulating her until coherent words were no longer possible.

He worked closer to the counter. Dorothea's legs lifted, and she put her feet on the edge so she was curled up and widely, wantonly exposed. Her groping fingers found his pants and began unbuttoning the fly. As she fumbled to free him, Fargo thought for the first time what might happen if anyone entered the store.

They would find something on the counter that wasn't for sale at any price.

He gasped when her fingers curled about his thick, meaty shaft. Stepping up so his legs rubbed against the lower portion of the counter, he bent forward as Dorothea lay back, supporting herself on her elbows. He moved forward, the tip of his manhood dragging across the damp region he had already explored with his finger.

Both of them groaned in pleasure. Then the groan turned to a gasp of delight as Fargo shoved his hips forward forcefully and buried himself deep into the lovely blonde's overheated interior. He wobbled then steadied himself when he felt the tightness surrounding him contract. He thought he had entered a mine shaft— and that it had collapsed on him.

But no mine shaft was ever so soft and yielding and exciting. He pulled back slowly until only a fraction of his length remained between her, then he thrust forward again. This scooted Dorothea across the counter. She grabbed the edge of the counter and pulled herself back, driving the pleasurable length of his manhood back where it excited them both the most.

Fargo bent over and kissed her breasts and throat and then brushed across her lips. Then he moved, his hips pistoning back and forth until all thought of doing anything else vanished from his mind. How he had missed Dorothea!

His loins ignited like wildfire. His muscles trembled and sweat poured down his body, as much from the stifling noonday heat as from the amorous activity in which he engaged. Fargo grabbed a handful of her womanly rump and pulled her forcefully toward his groin. This allowed him to bury himself even deeper. Then they began rotating their hips.

Dorothea went in one direction. Fargo went in the other. The increased friction and delicious movement was more than enough to push the woman over the edge of ecstasy. She cried out, her head rolling from side to side, causing a wild spray of lustrous blonde hair to float about her face.

Fargo tried to hang on, to push more. He thrust hard

a few more times, then erupted like a volcano. Through the haze of his own desire he heard Dorothea cry out again, then grow limp.

All too soon, passions spent, Fargo turned weak all over. He had been through so much during the prior week to exhaust him. Nothing he had done or that had been done to him was likely to be repeated. But being with Dorothea truly tuckered him out—yet he wanted more!

"You are a real stallion, Skye. Maybe you ought to go away for a while more often, if every homecoming is going to be like this."

"You'll put me into an early grave. I'm not sure my heart can stand exertion like this."

"Let's see!" she cried joyously, reaching for his limp organ, intending to coax it back to life.

"No, no, not right now. I've got business."

"You certainly gave *me* the business," Dorothea said wickedly. She smiled and Fargo almost relented. Then he knew he had to finish what he had promised Captain Chapman he would do.

"I need your help," he started.

"I should say so. It'd be a waste if you did any of this by yourself."

"Be serious," he chided. Gazing over at her nakedness, the way she was flushed and obviously wanting more, made it difficult to keep his mind on the situation at hand. "I need your help with your papa."

"With Papa? What do you mean?" She sat up, pulling on her sweaty blouse and hopped off the counter, rearranging her rumpled skirts.

"You know he's selling firewater. Taos Lightning. He's got to stop or the captain's going to lock him up."

"Oh, that. Why, Skye, that's not true. It's something Luella has been saying for months and months, as if she would care how Papa made his money. If she can spend it, she doesn't care where it comes from."

Fargo could see an answer as to why Luella Kincaide would take up with a man like Texas Jack Sawyer. This might be it. But why would the woman want his help stopping the illegal whiskey sales?

Unless . . .

"Luella asked me to stop your pa because I think Texas Jack told her to," Fargo said. "If the liquor got the Indians all fired up, it might make stealing women and children harder for him."

"Wait, stop, Skye. I don't know what you're saying."

He told her. As his story of how Sawyer supplied children to Benavidez to sell in Mexico unfolded, her eyes widened and she turned pale. Then Dorothea became angry.

"Why, that low-down, no-account sidewinder! I'll cut out his foul heart myself! How dare he do this to my sister!"

"I thought you didn't get along with Luella?" Fargo asked.

"I don't, but she's my sister after all!" Dorothea stormed about the store, banging pots and pans and stamping her foot. "Oh, Lu! How could you tie up with such a skunk?"

"First things first," Fargo said. "Stopping the whiskey trade will keep Captain Chapman from poking around too much more. Why he hasn't figured out that your father's the only one able to supply the whiskey is beyond me."

"The captain's sweet on me, that's why," Dorothea said. "He doesn't want to do anything to hurt me."

Everything fell into place for Fargo concerning Chapman's behavior. The captain wanted *him* to bring Austin Kincaide to justice, hoping this would sour any relationship he had with Dorothea. The captain could then gallop up on his horse, playing the role of the savior, and win the fair lady for his own. He wouldn't be the one accusing Austin Kincaide of bootlegging; it would be his scout. The captain could work out a deal getting Kincaide off, then ride away with Dorothea as his due for preserving her family and keeping her father out of prison.

"He won't do anything if the Taos Lightning stops flowing, especially to the Indians and to the soldiers at the fort."

"How could he?" muttered Dorothea, obviously

thinking of her father. "He's got a taste for the whiskey himself, but to sell it like this?" She shook her head. Dorothea looked at him and asked almost hesitantly, "Are you sure he is the one selling the liquor?"

"I saw it with my own eyes," Fargo said. "I was going to tend to the problem then but I got waylaid." He did not want to rehash all that had happened to him, from going into Canyon de Chelly after Broken Finger to the Navajo chief rescuing him from Benavidez's grip.

"Then let's not dally," Dorothea said firmly. "We can find Papa at home. The sooner he stops, the sooner we can get on to other things." Dorothea's blue eyes gleamed, leaving Fargo no doubt what she meant. If things settled down in New Mexico Territory there would be no need for him to go on long scouts, leaving time for other pursuits.

They left the general store, Dorothea closing the door and leaning a crude CLOSED sign against the outside. She bustled along, eager to get the confrontation with her father over. As they walked, Fargo looked around for any sign of Luella—or her fiancé. He had a score to settle with Texas Jack Sawyer.

Ojo del Oso slept quietly in the heat of the day, and Fargo saw no trace of the gambler or Dorothea's sister. They reached her father's house. She hesitated, then went inside. Fargo trailed behind, not sure if he ought to take the lead or let the woman do the talking. Coming from his daughter, the injunction against selling Taos Lightning might affect Austin Kincaide more.

"Dorothea, what are you doin' here?" asked the sutler. He was propped up in a chair, one leg hiked onto an ottoman. From the way he sat, the leg pained him. Fargo guessed the leg was not all there was giving the man considerable distress. Kincaide might actually have a conscience.

"I see you brought along Mr. Fargo. I'd heard he was on the outs with Chapman. What's happenin'?" Kincaide called.

"Papa, is it true?"

"What are you talkin' about, child?" The words were gentle, but Fargo saw the fright in the man's eyes.

"Are you selling that awful whiskey to the Indians and soldiers at the fort? It's got to stop. There is going to be a pile of trouble if you don't."

"You sound like you've upped and convicted me," he said sharply.

"I've seen you selling whiskey to a soldier. Corporal Anthony. Or should I say *Private* Anthony, since he got busted? I can ask any Pueblo Indian around where they get their booze. What do you think they'll tell me?"

"Liars! All them redskins are born liars!"

"Am I looking at another liar, Papa?" Dorothea asked. "Do you deny selling it?"

"No," he admitted grudgingly. "But I only sell it cuz I need the money. Sales to the fort are slow. That captain doesn't pay too promptly. And I need the whiskey for my own . . . use."

"Kills the pain, doesn't it?" asked Fargo. "What's your problem?"

"That's none of your business," snapped Kincaide.

"Well, Father, it is certainly *mine*!" cried Dorothea. "Are you ill?"

Austin Kincaide said nothing for a moment, then his face fell and all pretense vanished. "The doc says I've got a few months, no more. I wanted to lay up as much money as I could for you and Lu 'fore I cash in. And the whiskey, well, I need it to soften the pain."

"What is it?"

"Cancer," Austin Kincaide said. "Reckon it's all inside me, eatin' up everything. That's what it feels like. Mr. Fargo, you gonna stop me from bringin' in the Taos Lightning? It's about all that's strong enough to keep down the pain."

"I don't think Captain Chapman would have any problem with you bringing it in, but just for your own needs. No more selling to the soldiers. And certainly no more whiskey sales to the Indians."

"Dorothea, I'm so sorry. I had wanted to do more for you. A few hundred is all I got. It's not enough for a dowry for Lu, and it's certainly not enough to keep you going. You deserve so much more."

"I've got the store, Papa," she said. "Why didn't you

tell me?" She knelt beside him, took Kincaide's hand, and pressed it to her cheek.

Fargo backed away, letting them be alone. It wasn't his place intruding on them right now. Besides, he had Texas Jack Sawyer to find and shoot down like the dog that he was.

Fargo had to stop the gambler before he married Luella. It would be bad enough losing a fiancé. He didn't want her losing a husband and a father.

16

Fargo hunted through the sleepy town of Ojo del Oso for Texas Jack Sawyer but did not find the gambler anywhere. The barkeep in the Silver Centavo claimed not to have seen Sawyer in a week. From the way his eyes darted around like a trapped fawn, Fargo knew he was lying. Given time and the promise of imprisonment in the Fort Fauntleroy stockade, the bartender might be enticed to tell what he knew.

For his part, Fargo was getting tired of hunting Sawyer and wanted to end the matter. Find Sawyer, get evidence against Benavidez, and stop the slave trade. It seemed simple enough. Maybe too simple. The men had been trading in human flesh for some time and had kept free of the law. Until Chapman had arrived with orders to stamp out such doings in this part of the New Mexico Territory, they had free rein.

No longer.

Putting Benavidez in jail would cause *los ricos* to rise up and maybe force the poorer Mexican settlers to join them. This threat of a small range war bothered Fargo. He preferred to end Benavidez's odious trade without provoking the others. How to do it was something he had to play very carefully.

As he walked back down the dusty main street, he saw that the CLOSED sign on the general store had been taken down. The door stood ajar to allow some faint whiff of hot afternoon breeze to enter. Fargo doubted Dorothea had returned. She had much to talk with her father about. Poking his head into the dim, cool interior, he saw the counter where he and Dorothea had so amorously passed a few minutes earlier in the afternoon. The articles for sale they had knocked to the floor were once more on display.

"Anyone here?" he called out. Fargo rested his hand on his Arkansas toothpick, remembering he had given Broken Finger his Colt. He needed to buy a new six-shooter, but he was damned if he was going to buy a new Henry rifle. *That* he would get back from Sawyer or Benavidez—whichever of the slavers had it.

"Yes, in the back," replied a faint voice. For a moment he thought it might be Dorothea. Then Luella pushed aside the curtain and came into the main store, wiping her hands on her apron.

"Good afternoon," Fargo said, touching the dusty brim of his hat.

"Mr. Fargo," Luella said. "I did not expect to see you. Not after all I'd heard about your . . . dealings with Captain Chapman."

"It was a mistake," he said. "I'm here on official business."

"This is a strange place to go scouting," Lu said, putting the counter between them. She seemed as nervous as a long-tailed cat lying next to a rocking chair. Fargo wondered if she didn't like being so close to a jailbird, or if there was something more. He had no idea how much Texas Jack had told her about his dealings. Fargo had no idea how caught up in the gambler's illegal schemes Luella Kincaide might be. She could be responsible for goading him into the slave trade in the first place. A pretty girl like her might wrap a man around her little finger.

Fargo snorted, thinking how it was between him and Dorothea.

"I'm hunting down the men responsible for most of the slave trading," he said bluntly. "This might just be the best place to start."

"Why is that, sir?" she said in an icy tone. "Are you accusing me of something like that?"

"No, but you might know more than you're letting on. Your betrothed is responsible for kidnapping no fewer than a couple dozen youngsters and then selling them to Benavidez."

"That's absurd! Jack would never be involved in such a terrible thing," she said indignantly. There was a note of outrage in what she said, but Fargo heard something more, also. Perhaps Lu did not actually know, but only suspected? That might explain her reaction.

"I've seen him. And his gang. They moved on from robbing stages to trafficking in children."

"You don't know that. You . . . you're just being nasty because you don't like Jack!"

"You're right. I don't like him, but it's because of the way he deals in human flesh. Where is he?"

"Why should I tell you?"

"If he's innocent, he deserves a chance to clear his name. If he runs, everyone will know he's guilty."

"Why, I—" Lu sputtered for a moment. "I'm sorry I asked you for that favor."

"I've spoken with your father. He's not going to sell any more illegal whiskey. Your sister's with him right now."

"Dorothea." The woman sniffed. "I might have known. She was supposed to be tending the store. The last shipment from Santa Fé has to be put on the shelves and she's done none of it. She leaves it all for me to do, that lazy—"

"Texas Jack," Fargo cut in, getting her back to the question he wanted an answer to most. "Where is he?"

"I don't know," Lu said. "He left town a couple days ago. I wanted to go with him, but he said it was business. I assume he rode to Santa Fé, since he does most of his business there."

"Gambling business?"

"I couldn't say. Perhaps so, since that is how he makes his living."

"That and selling slaves to Benavidez," Fargo said, a steely edge to his words.

Luella slammed both hands flat on the counter and leaned forward. Her face flushed, and she almost gasped as anger seized her.

"Get out of this store and don't ever come back! I

137

don't care if Dorothea is sweet on you. I won't listen to your lies about Jack. He's a good man, and we're going to get married. You're not going to stop that, Mr. Fargo. I swear, you are not!''

Fargo turned and left the store, knowing he would find out nothing more from Luella Kincaide. Not by asking questions, at least. He ducked around the store and waited less than five minutes before the woman hurried out. She did not bother putting up the CLOSED sign. Luella came bustling out, looked around but did not see him, then almost ran down the street in the opposite direction.

If she had headed for the saloon, Fargo might have believed she had no idea where Texas Jack Sawyer was hiding. But Lu took off in the other direction, as if she knew he wasn't gambling away the afternoon in the Silver Centavo.

Fargo followed carefully since he did not want to spook her. She went to the livery stable and spoke with the owner, finally getting into a heated argument with the man. Fargo could not overhear the subject of the argument but thought it might have something to do with payment. Luella finally pointed into the stables and said something that soothed the man's ruffled feathers. He went around to the side of the livery and in a few minutes returned with a buggy for her.

Luella jumped in, grabbed the reins, and snapped the leather briskly to get the swaybacked horse moving. Fargo sauntered over. Following her in a buggy would be simple. She headed south out of Ojo del Oso. He knew the lay of the land well in that direction. If she tried to get off the road, she would break an axle fast. Wherever Texas Jack hid, it was somewhere near the main road.

"Howdy," the stable owner said when he saw Fargo. "What can I do for you?"

"Where's Miss Kincaide heading in such a hurry? I was supposed to give her a message from her pa."

"Can't rightly say," the man said, cocking his head to one side and eyeing Fargo suspiciously. "Weren't you locked up over at the fort? Heard tell you let that savage Broken Finger go scot-free."

"That was all a misunderstanding. I'm working for the captain again as a scout." Fargo frowned. Something was not right. Or rather, something *was* right and should not have been.

"I hear something inside," Fargo said, pushing past the man. He stopped just inside the door and stared. In a stall toward the rear of the stable stood a familiar sight.

"You interested in that horse? Make you a good price since them soldiers don't much like paints. Too easy for the Injuns to see."

"The Ovaro is mine," Fargo said. "Where'd you get it?"

"Yours? Well, now, that can't be. I swapped it for services."

"With Texas Jack Sawyer?"

"Well, yeah, it was that gambling man what brought the horse in. We swapped out what he owed me for the horse. And Miss Kincaide told me to take the buggy rental out of the price I make on sellin' the horse. It's a good one."

"It surely is," Fargo said, "and it's mine. Sawyer stole it from me."

"Now wait a minute. I'm not givin' you that horse on your say-so. Sawyer might be a tinhorn gambler but nobody's ever accused him of bein' a horse thief before."

"That's because he hasn't been in Ojo del Oso long enough," Fargo said. "Ask anyone at Fort Fauntleroy what I ride. Have them describe it real good for you. That's my horse." He went to the Ovaro, which nickered and shoved its muzzle into Fargo's hand.

"The horse has been mighty standoffish with everyone else," the liveryman said. "You got the touch."

"You've got my horse I tell you," Fargo said. "The one I rode into town on, not the one I came across out in the *malpais*."

"What would you need two horses for? That's a lot of feeding, and I don't reckon the captain pays a scout all that much."

Fargo saw what the man angled toward. He heaved a sigh and said, "You are right. Why would I need a second horse when my Ovaro is more than enough? What do you say if I left my other horse here? If you happen to sell it before I come back to claim it, more power to you."

"I'd have to see if the horse is in good condition," the man said. "Mostly though, one horse is as good as another out here. Too many of the men look at their mounts as possible food if the going gets too rough out in the desert."

Fargo made the exchange, giving the horse he had taken from Benavidez's vaquero to the liveryman and once more riding high and fancy free on his pinto. The Ovaro appreciated having its usual rider seated, and Fargo was glad to have the sturdy horse under him once more. Even better, amid his tack he found his trusty Henry. A quick check showed the rifle none the worse for having been taken by Texas Jack Sawyer.

Making sure the Ovaro was watered, Fargo rode south out of Ojo del Oso on Luella Kincaide's trail.

He had little trouble following the buggy, although the sun-baked road was hard as rock. One of the wheels wobbled slightly and made a distinctive pattern in the dirt. Moreover, Luella paid little attention to driving and wandered from one side of the road to the other, making it even easier for Fargo to see which way she rode.

As he made a sharp bend in the road, he heard the clatter of the iron-rimmed wheels against the rock ahead. Then there was silence. Fargo reined back and dismounted, advancing on foot to scout the road ahead. He cautiously looked around and saw Luella climbing down from the buggy. She tossed the reins aside, trusting the tired horse would not bolt or wander off. She hurried along a faint path and vanished into the rocks.

Sawyer could not be far off. Fargo knew Luella was not the kind to go hoofing it over the desert and through the rocky foothills for long. She had the look of a city girl about her, wanting comfort and avoiding any hardship she could. Fargo suspected that was Sawyer's appeal to her. He promised her fine clothes, ample food, and the good life—somewhere else.

Moving quietly, Fargo wended his way through the forest of boulders, avoiding the thorny cactus and low-growing bushes that snatched at his ankles. Even a small rustling noise might alert Sawyer or his men. Fargo hefted his Henry, wondering how many of the gang he had to face.

"What are you doing here?" yelled Sawyer's loud, angry voice.

"Jack!" cried Lu. "I had to see you. He . . . he's in town! I thought you said he was gone for good!"

"Who are you talking about?"

"Fargo! Skye Fargo!"

A long silence followed. Then Sawyer said, "That son of a bitch Benavidez was supposed to take care of him. He must have let him go."

"The captain put Fargo in the stockade for a while, because he had let the Navajo out. But he got out."

"You should have come to me sooner," Sawyer said, changing his tune entirely. "I could have done something about Fargo if he was rottin' away in the fort lockup."

"What are we going to do? Fargo was going on about getting Papa to stop dealing in the illegal whiskey."

"That much is good news for us," Sawyer said. "Your pa was drawing too much attention from the army. Having Chapman and his soldiers sniffing around like bloodhounds wasn't good for business."

"Business, Jack? What are you up to?"

Fargo's eyes widened in surprise. He had pretty well decided that Luella knew of her fiancé's slave trading ways. Now he heard that she was as much of a dupe as could be. Luella had wanted a man so badly she had ignored all the signs.

"I've told you. I have dealings with Benavidez and some others among *los ricos*. I trade for this and that. Nothing for you to worry your head over, especially now that the Taos Lightning has dried up."

"Why don't you want the army nosing around? What you're doing isn't legal, is it, Jack?" Lu paused and asked in a low voice, "You *are* trading in slaves, aren't you?"

"Of course he is," came a new voice. It took Fargo a second to recognize it. Villanueva. Fargo had suspected that the other ranchero was involved. Now he knew for sure. "You are a stupid cow."

"Hey, now, you take that back!" demanded Sawyer. "She's my woman, and you can't say things like that to her!"

Fargo edged around the rock to get a better view of the men he spied on. He clutched his Henry tightly, ready to use it if he faced only Villanueva and Sawyer.

He sucked in his breath. Villanueva had several men with him. Too many to hope to take them all and still keep his own battered hide unventilated by lead.

The best he could hope to do now was find out what new devilment the men were up to and let Captain Chapman handle it.

"Be quiet," Villanueva said, as if speaking to a barking dog. "You have done poorly, you and Benavidez. It is time to profit from the trading again. What are your plans for taking more slaves?"

"It's a good one," Sawyer said eagerly, ignoring the slight to Leulla Kincaide in his rush to brag about how clever he was. "We'll snatch a few women and kids from the Zuñis, then make it look like the Navajos are responsible. If the Navajos put up any fuss, we'll do the same with their women and children, making it appear like the Pueblo Indians are the raiders. They'll be at each other's throats and nobody'll ever think to look for us."

"Done well, it can work," Villanueva said, nodding in agreement with Sawyer's vile plan. "It is simple enough for even your feeble intellect to pull off."

"Look, I don't cotton much to you insultin' me or Miss Kincaide," Sawyer said.

"I do not care what you like, señor," Villanueva replied in his arrogant tone. "Other than your liking for money. That greed is what binds us together stronger than a blood oath. Deliver fifty women and children to me in prime condition and I will double the price Benavidez has been giving."

"Three hundred dollars each?"

Villanueva laughed harshly. "Benavidez has paid you only one hundred dollars a head. Do not think to cheat me, Señor Sawyer. You are not that smart."

"I'll get them for you by sundown tomorrow," Sawyer said, again ignoring the implied threat and the outright insult delivered by Villanueva.

Fargo listened hard to hear what Sawyer's plans were. Which Pueblo? Zuñi? Another? In Santo Domingo? Jemez? As he strained to overhear, a sixth sense warned him of danger. Fargo took a step forward, as if advancing toward Sawyer, then dropped to one knee and spun around, the muzzle of his rifle rising.

Above him on the rocks stood a vaquero, wrapped in a brightly colored serape. From underneath the blanket dangling over the man's broad shoulders flashed a blue-steel Colt. Fargo's reactions were a little faster and his aim was a lot better. The bullet from his Henry caught the vaquero square in the chest, sending him staggering back.

But as the vaquero fell from his perch atop the rock, his Colt fired into the air. The bullet blasted off a rock and whined its death song far off into the distance. Fargo doubted one rifle shot would have gone unnoticed. Two gunshots would draw the nearby slavers like buzzing flies to a newly dead carcass in the hot sun.

Fargo lit out, hunting for a hiding place among the rocks, even as excited shouts and sharp commands from both Villanueva and Sawyer to find and kill him echoed in the hills.

17

Fargo circled the rock where the vaquero sprawled spread-eagle on his back, his lifeblood running in a thick trickle down the stone to be sucked up by the thirsty sand. The surrounding black lava rock of the *malpais* afforded Fargo little cover. The jagged edges would cut and tear at his boots, preventing him from getting too far fast enough to matter. Already, sounds of the vaqueros coming for him filled the air.

He looked up at the top of the rock and a crazy scheme came to him. He scaled the rock and ripped at the dead vaquero's colorful serape, flinging it over his head and then tugging on the man's large-brimmed sombrero, covering his face. Fargo crouched down and clutched at his chest as if he had been wounded and tried to hold the serape away from his body like a curtain. He hoped the angle and the blocking serape were enough so that the approaching men could not see their dead amigo behind him.

"Where is Fargo?" called out Texas Jack Sawyer. The gambler waved his six-gun around wildly.

"There," Fargo grated out, pointing. "Shot me. Ran that way." He pointed into the jumble of rocks. He waited a moment to see if Sawyer bought his act.

He did.

"Come on, you lazy good-for-nothings," growled the gambler. "After him!"

The vaqueros behind Sawyer all plunged ahead into the rocky terrain, hunting for Fargo and never realizing he remained on the rock above them. Fargo kept a low profile, wishing he could strip off the vaquero's pants with the fancy silver conchas along the seams. All of Villanueva's men seemed to have a taste for the richly designed silver disks. Fargo had to content himself with pulling the bloody serape down to hide himself. The sombrero did a bit more to conceal his identity but he dared not look up.

"Are you all right?" demanded Sawyer as he passed by at Fargo's feet. The gambler paused and something seemed to alert him. For a heart-stopping second, Fargo worried the gambler had spotted the real vaquero's body.

"Winged me," Fargo said in a low, husky voice, hoping to disguise himself enough to get away.

"Go on back and tend the horses. We might have to take out after him. And watch out for Villanueva. Protect him real good, you hear? Don't let that murderin' owlhoot shoot your *patrón* like he did you."

"Sí," Fargo replied, remembering to throw in a little Spanish to maintain the illusion. He didn't catch Sawyer's reply as the man tramped after the vaqueros on their futile hunt for a man who was actually behind them.

Fargo slid the vaquero's body down the far side of the rock so that it was wedged between two boulders, then hastily covered it with a few limbs from a greasewood bush. He hurried to where the slavers had left their horses. If Fargo could spook the horses and strand Villanueva and the rest, he could be on his way back to Fort Fauntleroy to get Chapman before anyone knew what was going on.

He slowed and bent over, as if holding his chest when he saw Villanueva was not alone. Three vaqueros guarded him. All three had their six-shooters out and were waving them around dangerously. Fargo's hope for a quick, easy escape, maybe even with Villanueva as his prisoner, evaporated like steam in this hot New Mexico sun.

"Aquí!" ordered Villanueva, pointing to a spot in the shade near him. He rattled off a string of Spanish so fast Fargo caught only a word here and there. He kept playacting like he was wounded and collapsed where Vil-

lanueva had pointed. This seemed to satisfy the ranchero.

From his vantage point, Fargo overheard what the man planned for the women and children Sawyer was to supply him. Fargo knew Benavidez was an evil son of a bitch, but realized Villanueva was much worse. He cruelly used the slaves before sending them down into the heart of Mexico. Fargo made out only parts of Villanueva's boasts but figured that the buyers in Mexico needed a steady supply of slaves because so many died in the fields, mines, and brothels.

Fargo forced himself to keep from working his Henry around and killing Villanueva here and now. Only a sense of self-preservation kept him from taking the shot. There was no way he could escape the three wild men acting as Villanueva's bodyguard. Even if he killed them, too, Sawyer and the others would be on him fast.

If he died, the slaving would continue unabated. He had to get Chapman to round up the lot of them if there was ever to be peace in this part of the territory.

Fargo still weighed the odds of four fast shots. Then he pushed the notion aside when Sawyer and the rest of the vaqueros trooped back. Their exasperation at not finding their quarry was obvious from their expressions.

"Well?" Villanueva demanded angrily.

"He's like a ghost. I'll be damned if I can figure where he went. No tracks to be found anywhere, even considering this is the *malpais*."

"You will be damned even if you don't find his tracks," murmured Villanueva. Louder so that Sawyer could hear, he said, "Tell me about how many slaves you will deliver and when. We waste our time hunting for coyotes."

"Well, sir," Sawyer began, as if he were a trader trying to make a sale to a reluctant customer, "I intend to go into the Zuñi village about fifteen miles from here. Me and some of your boys will snatch what women we can— young ones, just like you like—and then leave a few broken Navajo arrows. Maybe we can find a Navajo brave and dry-gulch him on our way to the Zuñi pueblo.

Then we can leave the body behind just like he was killed during the raid."

"Very good," Villanueva said. "But only women? I need a dozen boys to work the fields. Perez needs some for his copper mines in La Barranca del Cobre, too. They must be sturdy, strong, able to work long hours with little food."

"Well, señor, I reckon I can check their teeth and fetlocks like I would a horse I was plannin' to buy," Sawyer said sarcastically. "We take what we can take. The Injuns are gettin' riled and might pose a problem if we get too choosey."

"I will need far more than you delivered last time," Villanueva insisted.

"You'll get them," Sawyer promised.

The vaqueros went over to their horses and mounted. Fargo wasn't sure what he was supposed to do. He couldn't let them find out he was impersonating their dead amigo, not with so many of them all around. Yet he did not want to let Sawyer go off on his raid. There wasn't time to get word to the fort and have Captain Chapman field a company of cavalry to stop the slavers. Whatever was going to be done, he had to do by himself.

"You all right?" Sawyer asked. It took Fargo a second to realize that the gambler spoke to him. Fargo nodded, keeping the brim of the sombrero down low. "Then come on along with me."

Something in the man's tone turned Fargo wary. He nodded again. He had no idea which horse to mount so he hung back until it became apparent that the one remaining had to belong to the dead vaquero. Fargo mounted and hunched over, keeping the sombrero pulled low and the serape wrapped tightly around him. He tried to hang back but found himself pushed suddenly to the front of the raiding party.

Sawyer and Villaneuva spoke heatedly for another minute, then the gambler mounted, rode through the crowd of vaqueros, and came up beside Fargo.

"That way," Sawyer said, glowering. "You just took a bullet to the gut, not your head. Get a move on!"

Fargo had no idea where they headed. This must have

147

been discussed before he had shot the vaquero. He purposely rode at an angle, always heading back toward Sawyer, letting the gambler put more and more distance between them. Soon Fargo brought up the rear, eating trail dust and not minding.

He argued with himself over breaking away and heading out for Fort Fauntleroy and continuing with Sawyer to stop the raid. Somehow, the decision was made for him. Fargo found himself keeping up and even anticipating how the fight would go when they reached a Zuñi encampment a couple of miles away from a pueblo.

For all of Sawyer's bragging about bushwhacking a Navajo brave and leaving his dead body as proof that the raid had been committed by the rival tribe, he made no effort to find a warrior. They rode directly for the pueblo, reaching it at twilight. This suited Fargo just fine, giving him the added anonymity of shadow.

"All right, men, get yourselves ready. We can swoop down and snatch a dozen or more before they know we're a'comin'."

Fargo noticed that something was wrong. It took him a couple of seconds to figure out what it was. There was no reason for Zuñis to camp this close to their pueblo. That meant the vaqueros were not attacking Zuñis but some other Indian encampment.

And Fargo thought he knew whose it might be.

"Go get 'em!" cried Sawyer, whipping out his six-gun and leading the way. Fargo lit out after him, fell back, confused. The vaqueros were already rounding up children and a few women. From what Fargo could tell, they were Zuñis. His carefully thought-out reasons that this could not possibly be a Zuñi camp were dashed as boy after boy was tied up and slung over horses.

Fargo knew it was now or never. He was no back-shooter, but he could not permit the vaqueros to take so many prisoners. Riding up behind one vaquero, Fargo swung his rifle. The steel barrel caught the man on the back of his exposed neck, stunning him. A second swing sent him crashing to the ground where he stirred feebly.

"What's goin' on?" demanded Texas Jack Sawyer.

This time Fargo fired his Henry. The rifle spat a foot-long tongue of orange flame in the dim twilight. But even as he pulled the trigger, he knew he had missed his target. Sawyer was already putting his spurs to his nervous horse, hightailing it from the camp at this sign of trouble.

Fargo spun around and saw the vaqueros turning on him. He returned fire and took one rider from the saddle. Another's horse reared, throwing him. Then Fargo reached over and freed several of the Zuñi children.

"Help the others get away!" he ordered them. They stared at him with wide, black suspicious eyes. Fargo shooed them on.

A bullet whizzed past his head, putting a hole in the stolen sombrero. Fargo threw the bulky hat into the night, momentarily drawing fire. He took out another vaquero with a round, not killing him but wounding him badly enough in the shoulder that he could not fire at Fargo.

The confusion in the camp masked details Fargo tried to understand. It looked as if the Zuñis were already tied up and the vaqueros had simply grabbed them—trading one set of captors for another.

Fargo sank low and hugged his horse's neck. He wished he had his Ovaro with him, but there was nothing he could do about that right now. If he had ridden the distinctively marked horse, Sawyer and the others would have known right away he was not their amigo.

He spurred the horse out of the camp, circled around and shot another vaquero from the saddle. But others joined the battle, and Indians came out of the dark like shadows, growing hands holding rifles and bows with nocked arrows.

Fargo had done all he could to free the Zuñi children. He turned his horse in the direction Sawyer had ridden, hoping to overtake the gambler and remove him from the earth once and for all. Let Luella Kincaide wear widow's weeds. Sawyer's death would benefit everyone else in New Mexico Territory.

And after Fargo took out Texas Jack, he could move on to Villanueva and Benavidez and the other corrupt *los ricos*.

The moon was not up yet and the ground looked like a calm black sea. Fargo slowed and then had to dismount to study the sun-baked ground for tracks. He was a good tracker—there were none better—but he had a devil of a time finding any clear trail to follow. Then he got lucky. Texas Jack Sawyer rode up onto a rise a quarter mile off and momentarily blocked the stars, appearing to be an inky ghost in the darkness.

Fargo swung back into the saddle and made a beeline for the rise. Sawyer vanished, but Fargo knew he had the gambler dead to rights. Sawyer was not the rider Fargo was and his horse flagged quickly because the man stupidly tried to push it far too long. In less than twenty minutes, Fargo closed the gap between him and the gambler.

"Who's back there?" cried Sawyer. His horse stumbled and almost threw him. He reined up as Fargo rode even closer, wary now because Sawyer was going to shoot rather than parley.

That suited Fargo just fine.

He laid the Henry rifle across the saddle in front of him, but from the trouble Texas Jack Sawyer had controlling his horse, the target might be too erratic for accurate shooting.

"Who's there?" repeated Sawyer. Then the gambler slid from the saddle, twisting his ankle as he jumped back from his crow-hopping horse and sitting down hard. Sawyer yelped, having fallen into a patch of prickly pear cactus.

"Who's here?" Fargo asked coldly as he rode up, his rifle pointed at the struggling gambler. "Your worst nightmare."

"Don't shoot! Don't kill me!" Sawyer wiggled and squirmed and got out of the cactus, but the spines remained sticking in his butt. This thought stayed Fargo from shooting him. Sawyer would suffer more walking back to Fort Fauntleroy with all the nettles in his rump than he ever would by taking a bullet in his foul black heart.

Maybe Fargo could even persuade Captain Chapman to hang the son of a bitch.

Justice would be done that way—legally.

Other ideas then hit Fargo. Bringing charges against *los ricos* was hard. He had found that out trying to stop Benavidez. Going after a man like Villanueva would be even harder . . . unless a witness came forward to testify. A witness like Texas Jack Sawyer.

"Start walking," Fargo said.

"What are you going to do with me?"

"Make you testify."

"I can do that. I *want* to! They forced me to—"

"Shut up or I'll change my mind," Fargo said.

"You're a fair man, I can see that. I—"

"Shut up!"

Sawyer's head bobbed up and down. He started in the direction indicated by Fargo's rifle muzzle. Fargo smiled a little when he saw how gingerly Sawyer stepped, how he tried to pluck the spines from his worthless hide, how he would be completely tuckered out by the time they reached Fort Fauntleroy.

They backtracked toward the spot where Fargo had shot the vaquero on the rock. He wanted his Ovaro back under him. And in a way, he wanted to see how tortured Sawyer would be having to ride rather than hoof it. More than this, though, Fargo felt the pressure of time upon him. The sooner Sawyer told Chapman everything he knew about the slave trade, the sooner it could be stopped.

Fargo grinned ear to ear when he saw his Ovaro standing patiently where he had left it. The horse had been left alone for a long time but had not tried to run off. A quick look at the stars told him it would soon be dawn.

Dropping to the ground, Fargo walked over to his horse and patted its head. Then he froze when he heard a six-shooter cock.

Turning slowly, Fargo saw Broken Finger sitting in shadow. The six-gun was the same Colt he had given the Navajo chief. And the weapon was pointed at him.

"You'd shoot me with my own pistol?" Fargo asked.

"No, I will kill your prisoner," Broken Finger said. "He tried to steal the Zuñi slaves I had taken."

Everything fell into place for Fargo. The Zuñis in the camp had been Navajo prisoners. The Navajos had been out rounding up more slaves when Sawyer and the vaqueros had attacked, stealing children already stolen from their pueblo and not knowing it.

"I need him," Fargo said. "Killing him won't do any good. Letting the army have him will stop the Zuñi raids on your people. It'll also stop *los ricos* from taking your women and children."

"He must die for all he has done. He was the one who kidnapped my son. For that, if nothing else, he will die."

Broken Finger pointed the Colt straight at a terrified Texas Jack Sawyer and Fargo was helpless to stop the killing.

18

"You'll make everything worse, Broken Finger, not better," Fargo said. "Kill him and the slave trade goes on. I need him—*we* need him—to testify."

"I'll say anything you want!" cried Sawyer. "You weren't mixed up in it, no sir, no way. It was all the doin' of them Mexicans. The rich ones. *Los ricos.* I know all about Benavidez's contacts down in Mexico. And Villanueva's, too."

"Shut your mouth, already," Fargo said. Something in his tone and expression caused Broken Finger to laugh. This eased the tension. The Navajo chief lowered his Colt.

"What will happen if they no longer steal our women and children?" asked Broken Finger.

"That'll be it. You can vanish into Canyon de Chelly and live your lives in peace. Grow peaches on those fine fruit trees I saw," Fargo said. This caused Broken Finger to grow rigid, so Fargo backed off. Fargo had to keep telling himself that white men simply didn't mosey into Canyon de Chelly, look around like tourists, and then leave alive. This was a matter of pride and security for the Navajos. Dinetah was *their* land.

"What of the Zuñis and the other Pueblos?" asked Broken Finger. "Will they still raid?"

"They'll try. But if Captain Chapman doesn't have to deal with the politics and money of the Mexican settlers, he'll patrol more often and keep those raids to a minimum." Fargo saw the crafty look on Broken Finger's face. "That means you won't be allowed to go slave hunting, either."

"We can live without the lazy Zuñi slaves. And the Acoma and Santa Domingos, too," declared Broken Finger. "Utes make better slaves, anyway."

"Come on back to Fort Fauntleroy with me and let Chapman write up a treaty," Fargo said. At least he could see the end of the fighting and killing among the Navajos and the Pueblo.

"How long will the treaty last?"

"As long as both sides follow the rules. I'm no statesman to draw up such things. You'll have to rely on Captain Chapman for the details, but he is an honorable man."

"I am honorable, too," Broken Finger said, pounding his chest proudly. He handed back Fargo's Colt.

"Then there will be peace in New Mexico Territory," Fargo said.

Broken Finger paused a moment, then said, "There will be peace—until the white man breaks the treaty again."

To that, Fargo had no answer.

"You've done wonders, Mr. Fargo. I must say I did not believe you would accomplish anything."

Fargo saw the patrol returning, with both Benavidez and Villanueva in custody. Trailing them was a veritable mob of vaqueros, all grumbling and making threats. With Texas Jack Sawyer testifying against them, Fargo knew they would not escape justice this time.

Or would they? He heard Chapman speaking heatedly with Broken Finger.

"I cannot do that, Chief Broken Finger," Chapman said. "Torturing them to death is not allowed by our laws."

"Then let me do it," the Navajo insisted.

"Truth to the tell, I'll count myself lucky to send those rascals back to Mexico," Chapman said. This quieted Broken Finger. Fargo wondered at it, then decided the Navajo might consider an ambush along the long Jornado del Muerto trail leading down into Mexico.

Things worked out for the best. Already the fighting between the Pueblos and the Navajos had quieted.

A shrill voice caused him to turn. Luella Kincaide rushed up, her fingers curled into claws.

"There you are, you miserable cur!" It took Fargo a few seconds to realize she meant him. "You framed him! You forced Jack to lie! They'll kill him for sure."

He caught her right hand as she tried to scratch out his eyes. Holding Lu tightly, he glared at her until she subsided.

"He's alive. Sawyer might do time in the territorial penitentiary for everything he's done, but he's alive when I could have killed him. And Lord knows I wanted to."

"You, you—" Luella Kincaide sputtered, then jerked free and hurried over to the stockade to speak with Texas Jack again. Fargo had not made friends with her, but he had not intended to. She had hitched her wagon to a dubious stallion. It was Luella's fault if the horse didn't take her where she thought she might.

"I think Broken Finger will honor the treaty," Chapman said, walking up. He eyed Luella Kincaide and shrugged off the woman's ire. "You put a stopper in the illicit whiskey trade, too. I have not had a single drunken soldier since you, uh, dealt with the matter."

"You might consider getting Mr. Kincaide to import some Taos Lightning legally. All the saloon sells is that bitter witch's brew they call beer. A touch of whiskey now and then isn't such a bad thing," Fargo said. "But keep an eye on him."

"I don't know about that," Chapman said, frowning. "It's hard enough dealing with that saloon. I've never caught anyone there selling to troopers or Indians but . . ."

"The Silver Centavo's easy enough to police," Fargo said. "Just watch for the illicit sales out the back door. It'll go a ways toward keeping your men in line if they can get a legal drink—but not too much—now and then."

"I will consider that," Chapman said, obviously distracted. The captain appeared uneasy and unsure of himself. Fargo knew why.

"Captain, I've been thinking. The reasons you hired

155

me to scout for you are all gone. I might stick around a spell, but I'd get mighty bored. Why don't we settle up so I can find something more to my liking than garrison duty?"

Chapman's shoulders lost their tension and a smile danced on his lips.

"I'll miss you, Fargo. I really will." He thrust out his hand. Fargo shook with him, knowing the captain was lying through his teeth. He wouldn't miss Skye Fargo at all.

"You really have to go, Skye?" Dorothea asked. She rolled onto her back and put her hands behind her golden-tressed head. This caused the sheets to slip down her sleek, naked body. He looked from her comely face to the twin mounds of her breasts, now well kissed after their fierce lovemaking.

"You pa's going to be hailed as a hero for putting an end to the illegal liquor flooding the area."

"But Luella's all mad that Texas Jack is in the stockade and likely to do time in the territorial prison over in Las Vegas," Dorothea said. "Not that he doesn't deserve it—and more."

Fargo did not offer his opinion that Sawyer ought to have his neck stretched along with Benavidez and Villanueva. He took in the sight of her naked body for what he knew would be the last time. He really did have to ride on, but this had been about the finest send-off he'd ever received, bar none.

"What about me, Skye? Are you going to leave me all by my lonesome?"

"Things have a way of working themselves out," he told her.

"I like it better when your thing works its way into me," she said mischievously, rolling onto her side and digging under the bedclothes. Fargo grunted when she found his exhausted organ and began working some life back into it.

From outside came the sound of a horse trotting up.

Fargo pushed her hand away and said, "You've got company. Better go see who it is."

"Oh, bother," Dorothea said, but she was already out of bed and slipping into her clothing. Fargo watched her for a moment, then hurriedly dressed. He pulled on his boots and settled his gun belt at his waist.

Dorothea paused at the door leading from the bedroom and blew him a kiss. Then she went to answer the knock at the door.

Fargo moved so that he could see who was calling. Standing in the doorway, a cluster of wildflowers in his hand, Captain William Chapman looked like an uneasy schoolboy stopping by to court his sweetheart.

"Miss Kincaide, I've come to pay my respects." He held out the flowers to her.

Fargo did not wait around to hear what Dorothea said to her new beau. He wished them both well. It had been apparent to him how relieved Chapman had been when Fargo had announced that he was riding on.

Going out the narrow bedroom window, Fargo dropped to the hard ground behind the small house. He swung up into the saddle and turned the Ovaro's face toward the north. It had been a spell since he had seen Denver City, and he had heard exciting things were happening there.

And if they weren't, he'd find some other place. Somewhere beyond the distant horizon.

LOOKING FORWARD!
The following is the opening
section from the next novel in the exciting
Trailsman series from Signet:

THE TRAILSMAN # 228

WYOMING WAR CRY

*Wyoming, 1861—where greed and savagery
run rampant, and the prairie runs red
with the blood of innocents. . . .*

The tall rider in buckskins reined up on a low rise and
surveyed the prairie ahead. The trail he was following
featured something new: a squat building of sod and
wood that boasted a rickety corral and a water trough.
The rider's lake-blue eyes narrowed, taking in a trio of
dusty horses tied to a long hitch rail, and a crudely
painted sign that read: HONEST JACK'S TRADE AND
LIQUOR EMPORIUM.

Excerpt from WYOMING WAR CRY

Skye Fargo had half a mind to avoid the hovel. He had seen countless others like it in his travels. Dens of iniquity, a parson would brand them, full of sundry two-legged sidewinders better left alone. But Fargo had never minded a little iniquity now and then, and the presence of four wagons parked out front sparked his curiosity. Lightly touching his spurs to his pinto stallion, he trotted on down the rise and over to the rail.

Nearby was a covered wagon. Not a full-size Conestoga, but a smaller model, about half as big, and from what Fargo could tell, crammed with various tools. The other three wagons were actually vans, similar to those the army used to transport the wounded, only these had the words WESTERN UNION TELEGRAPH COMPANY stenciled on their sides.

Dismounting, Fargo looped the Ovaro's reins around the rail and moved toward the door. As he did, a short figure came bustling around the last van and nearly collided with him.

"Hey! Watch where you're going, you big ox!"

Fargo looked down into a dirt-streaked face framed by a floppy brown hat that covered close-cropped black hair. A baggy shirt and even baggier pants hung in folds on a bony youth who wasn't more than eighteen or nineteen, and didn't stand much over five feet in height. Dark eyes flared with resentment, and small hands balled into fists.

"The least you could do is apologize, mister. What is it with you frontier clods? There isn't one of you who has the manners of a goat." Although the youth didn't have a whisker on his chin, his voice was low and deep. Uncommonly so, Fargo thought. "I have half a mind to thrash you."

Fargo laughed out loud. He couldn't help himself. The chances of that happening were about the same as a buffalo sprouting wings and flying. "Simmer down, runt. You're the one who almost bumped into me."

"Is that a fact?" Bristling, the youth cocked a fist as if he fully intended to throw a punch.

"And as far as manners go," Fargo said good-naturedly, "it's a case of the pot calling the kettle black."

The youth's mouth fell. "Why, you son of a—!" he blurted, and started to swing, but just then someone flew past Fargo and grabbed the hothead's arm.

"Wood Carrington! What in the world do you think you're doing? Get a grip on that temper of yours! You're liable to cost us our jobs."

The newcomer was barely a year older than the first youth, and wore nearly identical clothes—the same sort of floppy hat, the same exceptionally baggy shirt and britches. His face was also splashed with grime, but his eyes were green, not brown, and he averted Fargo's glance. "Sorry, mister. Pay my brother no mind."

"Wood?" Fargo repeated. "Is that his name or what he has between his ears?"

"Damn you!" Wood spat, and would have torn into Fargo if not for his older brother, who pushed him back against the van. "Let go of me, Darr! We can't let ruffians like him talk to us like that!"

"Yes, we can," Darr said. Gripping Wood by both shoulders, Darr shook him as a parent might a misbehaving child. "Listen to me! We have to accept some changes. We're not east of the Mississippi anymore."

"No man can talk to me like that and walk away standing!" Wood huffed.

"Things aren't what they used to be, remember? We have to deal with them on their terms, not ours."

Fargo thought he understood and added his two bits. "Your brother has a point. Out here there are men who will shoot you if you so much as look at them crosswise. Never start a fight you can't finish."

"Better yet," Darr said to his sibling, "never start a fight, period. We can't afford the grief it would bring down on our heads. Understand?"

Wood, sulking, nodded.

"That's a good idea," Fargo complimented Darr,

"especially if you're not going to go around heeled." Neither of the youths wore revolvers. Or, for that matter, carried any weapons whatsoever. "Maybe you should buy yourselves a couple of knives."

"No need," Darr said, releasing his brother. "Some of the men in our party have guns. They'll protect us if we run into danger."

"Your party?" Fargo glanced at the van. "The two of you work for the telegraph company?"

"We string line for them, yes." Darr began to smooth his rumpled shirt, then, oddly, jerked his hands down. "We're to help push the telegraph clear to California by the end of the year, if not sooner. In case civil war breaks out."

"Do tell," Fargo said. He'd heard rumors war was imminent but nothing about the telegraph.

"Don't you read the newspapers?" Wood asked sarcastically.

"Behave," Darr said.

Wood ignored his brother. "Our country is growing by leaps and bounds, mister. Thirty-one million, that's how many people we have now. Pretty soon there won't be room for bumpkins like you."

"Oh, there's plenty of room," Fargo said. He should know. His wide-flung gallivanting had taken him from Canada to Mexico, from the muddy Mississippi to the far-off Pacific coast. Few Easterners truly appreciated how vast the country was, and how much of it had yet to be explored, much less settled.

"In twenty years there won't be," Wood crowed. "People will come flocking west, and before you know it, there will be as many towns and cities as there are back East. The days of the redskin and uncouth louts like you are numbered."

In that, Fargo reflected, the youth might well be right. The California gold rush and the boom of emigrants along the Oregon Trail were proof the States were bursting at the seams. But where Wood saw the exodus as progress, Fargo saw it as a plague of locusts about to sweep over the land, devouring everything in their path.

Darr was speaking. "Again, I apologize for my brother, mister. He's always been rather opinionated."

"Bullheaded, is more like it," Fargo said. "Keep a tight rein on him, or one of these days his opinions will be the death of him."

Wood stiffened. "Was that a threat?"

Fargo was tired of the boy's antics. "No, a prediction." Wheeling, Fargo strode indoors, stopping just inside so his eyes could adjust to the gloom, and his nose to the stink.

The Emporium reeked of must and sweat and whiskey and other odors better left unidentified. To the left was the dry-goods section, four measly shelves stacked with barely enough housewares to fill a cupboard. To the right were several tables and a long plank bar. Behind it, neatly arranged, were enough liquor bottles to satisfy the needs of the entire Sixth Cavalry.

The proprietor, Honest Jack, was a portly fellow with a belly as big as a stove and a head as bald as marble. He wore shabby clothes and an apron that hadn't been cleaned since the turn of the century. Smiling broadly, he beckoned and said, "Howdy, stranger. What's your poison?"

Fargo ambled over, aware that three grungy characters at a corner table were taking his measure. He returned the favor. One was a hulking brute in a heavy buffalo-hide coat, the other a swarthy breed with a nasty scar on his cheek, and the third a pasty-faced weasel who wore two guns, strapped low.

The other patrons, seven men lining the bar, Fargo rated as no threat. They were drinking and laughing and joking. Western Union workers, Fargo guessed. Angling past them to the end of the plank, he stood so a wall was behind him. Old habits were hard to break.

The barkeep ambled over. "You still haven't said what you'd like, stranger. I've got it all. Whiskey, scotch, bourbon, rum. Hell, I even have a bottle of wine for those with sissified taste."

"Coffin varnish will do me fine," Fargo said.

"One whiskey, coming right up."

The door opened and shafts of sunlight speared the floorboards. In walked Darr and Wood, their hat brims pulled low. They moved to a table near Fargo and sat with their backs to the others.

A gray-haired character at the bar shifted toward them. He had chipmunk cheeks, a bulbous nose, and a kindly expression. "Don't you boys care to partake? It'll be a spell before we get to drink again."

"Not until we reach Fort Laramie," added a spindly individual at his side, a scarecrow in homespun with an Adam's apple the size of a melon.

"No, thank you, Mr. Melton," Darr told the kindly old-timer. "We don't fancy hard drink all that much."

"Are you addlepated?" Melton joked. "Liquor is God's gift to all us fools and sinners."

"Not only that," the scarecrow added, "it puts hair on a fella's chest."

"How would you know, Charlie?" Melton said. "Your chest is as bare as a baby's bottom."

At that, the entire telegraph crew cackled.

Only Fargo saw the three men at the corner table exchange glances. And he was the only one who saw the weasel in the black hat and vest rise and strut toward the brothers, thumbs hooked in his gunbelt. As casually as could be, Fargo lowered his right hand to his side.

"So you two boys don't like to drink?" the weasel declared, dripping with scorn. "Where are you brats from, anyhow, that they don't teach you proper?"

Darr and Wood looked up. "Keep your ugly nose out of our business, mister," the latter answered.

The two-gun man stopped cold. "Better watch that mouth of yours, sonny, or you'll bite off more than you can chew."

Darr came to his brother's defense again. "He didn't mean no insult. Don't hold it against him."

Melton took a step toward their table but froze when

the hardcase in the black vest dropped a hand to a polished gun butt. "They're just boys, friend. Fresh off the farm. They don't know any better."

From the table in the corner came a hearty guffaw, a slow, mocking laugh from the barrel chest of the hulking brute in the buffalo coat. "You hear that, Brody? Green as grass. Maybe the sprouts need to be clipped down to size."

"I hear, Angus. I hear," Brody said, sneering at the youths.

Melton and the Western Union men at the bar swapped worried looks. Melton stepped toward the gunman, smiling to show his intentions were friendly. "Listen, mister. We're not looking for trouble. We're on our way to Fort Laramie, and from there we'll be helping extend the telegraph line west."

"Is that a fact?" Brody said.

Melton moved between the hardcase and the table. "We've been on the go all day and we're bushed. I thought it would be nice to have a couple of drinks before we make camp for the night. I'm in charge of this crew."

"Who gives a damn?"

The foreman was no fool. Nervously licking his lips, he tried once more to make peace. "We'll be on our way, if it's all right with you. There's still another hour or so of daylight left, and it would be a shame to waste it." Melton gestured at the men at the bar and at the two brothers, motioning for them to get out of there.

Brody's hand shot out, lightning quick, gripping Melton by the shirt. "You'll leave when I say you can leave and not before, you old geezer."

Fargo looked at the proprietor, who showed no interest in intervening. Honest Jack had brought a glass over and was pouring three fingers of whiskey. "You're not going to do anything?" Fargo asked quietly so no one else would overhear.

"Are you loco?" Honest Jack whispered. "Buck Frank Brody?" I might as well bait a wolverine in its den. He's snake mean, mister." Jack leaned forward.

"Him and his partners, Angus Stark and Pawnee Tom, have been hanging around for days now, making my life miserable. They picked on a drummer yesterday. Made the poor cuss eat a pair of socks he was selling. The guy about choked to death."

Brody had pushed Melton aside and was glaring at the brothers. "What will it be, brats? You can eat crow or you can be carried out of here."

Darr began to rise but stopped when Brody tensed as if to draw. "Look, this is ridiculous. Why can't we handle this like adults?"

Angus Stark's hearty mirth rose to the rafters. "He's callin' you immature, Brody. Sayin' you're more of a kid than he is."

"Is that so?" The gunman strutted nearer, his spurs jangling.

"I said no such thing," Darr responded, shoving himself erect. "And I'll be darned if we're going to sit here and be made laughingstocks." He tugged at his brother's sleeve but Wood wouldn't budge.

"You'll be *darned,* huh?" Brody said, mimicking the younger man's tone and inflection. "Mercy me, but you brats sure do use hard language."

Angus and Pawnee Tom roared with laughter but no one else joined in. Frank Brody, cocky as a bantam rooster, swaggered right up to their table. "Maybe I should wash both your mouths out with soap."

Wood snapped. Beet red with anger, he came up out of his chair and jabbed a finger at Brody. "I'd like to see you try, you uppity wretch! You would be in for the shock of your worthless life."

Brody's mouth became a thin slit. "I would, would I?" He sidled to the left so he was facing them. "You're the one in for a shock, mealy mouth. Get down on your knees and beg me to spare you or I'll pistol-whip you within an inch of your life."

"I'd die first!" Wood said.

"Hush, will you?" Darr beseeched his kin, then sank

onto a knee, facing Brody. "How about if I do it instead? Here, I'm begging for our lives. I'm pleading with you to let us go our way in peace."

"You don't sound sincere enough," Brody said.

Fargo had witnessed enough. Pivoting so his left elbow was on the counter and his right hand was brushing his Colt, he said calmly, "That's enough fun for one day. Let the boys be."

Brody had the posture of a rattler about to strike. He flicked Fargo a look of annoyance and rasped, "This doesn't concern you, mister."

"I say it does."

Angus and Pawnee Tom stood and crossed toward their companion, Angus cradling a Sharps in the crook of his left elbow, Pawnee Tom fingering the hilt of a Bowie in a beaded-leather sheath on his right hip. The half-breed wore buckskin leggins and knee-high moccasins, also elaborately beaded.

"I pegged you as a busybody the second I saw you," the big buffalo hunter addressed Fargo. "Some folks just don't know when to leave well enough alone."

At long last Honest Jack spoke up. "Now, hold on there, fellas. I don't cotton to gunplay in my establishment. Something is bound to get busted, and my liquor and trade goods don't grow on trees."

"Shut up, you spineless yack," Angus said.

"Yes, sir," Honest Jack bleated.

Fargo focused on Frank Brody. When the violence erupted, Brody would make the first move. Fargo had met others like him, cocky coyotes who acted as if they owned the world, cruel bastards who took great delight in causing others pain and misery. "I'll only say this once. Leave now, and no one need be hurt."

Angus snorted. "Damned generous of you, mister, considering we outnumber you three to one."

"He's bluffing," Brody said. "Ain't no way in hell he can take all of us. Not all of us, he can't."

Darr was still on one knee. Abruptly standing, he went

to move between Fargo and the gunman. "You gentlemen can't be serious! You wouldn't really shoot one another over such a trifle, would you? That would be barbaric."

Angus gave the youth a shove that flung Darr onto the table. Darr would have tumbled off the other side had Wood not caught hold of him.

"Keep out of this, boy," the buffalo hunter snapped.

Pawnee Tom was craftily edging to the left so he would have a clear throw. He stopped when Fargo glanced at him.

Frank Brody's mouth creased in an arrogant smirk. "So how should we go about it, Angus? Do we let the breed whittle this jasper down to size with his pigsticker, or should I do the honors?" Brody chuckled, the sound like flint grating on steel. "I think it should be me. I ain't shot anyone in pretty near a month."

Fargo didn't bother replying. He had said his piece. Now the outcome was up to the three cutthroats. They would get to it eventually. Just as four-legged wolves sometimes had to work themselves into a killing frenzy before attacking moose or elk, the two-legged variety often needed to bolster their own backbone with boasts and threats.

The scarecrow at the bar, Charlie, slapped down his glass and rotated toward the entrance. "Enough of this! Let's head out before one of us takes a slug by mistake."

Brody glowered at him. "String bean, if you take a bullet, it won't be by accident. I'm shoot you plumb between the eyes if you so much as take a step."

Gulping, Charlie transformed into a statue. "Western Union warned us about savages and wild critters and the elements. But they never said anything about situations like this."

The big buffalo hunter chuckled. "Where in hell do you reckon you are, pilgrim? New York City? Out here a gent can cut his throat with his own tongue if he ain't powerful careful."

"It's silly," Darr said.

"It's stupid," was Wood's opinion.

"It's how things are," Brody corrected them both, and just like that, while everyone was distracted by their chatter, he went for his pistols, his hands swooping down and palming the matched set of nickel-plated Remingtons. He thought his ruse had worked. He thought he had Fargo dead to rights, and as he leveled the revolvers, he grinned.

Pawnee Tom was grinning, too, as his right hand flashed to his Bowie and he whipped the knife in an overhand throw.

Fargo exploded into motion, the Colt materializing as if it had leaped into his hand of its own accord. It boomed once, and Frank Brody tottered. It boomed twice, and the gunman was slammed backward as if smashed by an invisible fist and became entangled with a chair.

As the bantam gunny toppled, Fargo pivoted. Pawnee Tom's arm was at the apex of its swing. Another instant, and he would release the Bowie.

Fargo fanned the Colt, a trick he seldom resorted to unless at close range and he needed to get off a shot quickly.

Two swift blasts raised Pawnee Tom onto the tips of his toes. Like melted wax oozing down a candle, the half-breed seeped to the floor in a heap.

Fargo swung the Colt toward the buffalo hunter and thumbed back the hammer. The click was unnaturally loud in the sudden stillness. "How about you?"

Angus Stark hadn't so much as twitched a muscle. Tearing his eyes from his fallen friends, he grinned at the wisps of smoke curling from the muzzle of Fargo's six-shooter. "Whooee! That was some shootin', mister. I ain't seen the like in all my born days."

"You can see it again if you want," Fargo said.

"No, sir. Not here. Not now." With exaggerated slowness, the buffalo hunter laid the big Sharps down on a table and stepped back with his calloused hands in the air. "My momma didn't raise no simpletons."

Excerpt from *WYOMING WAR CRY*

Melton and the rest of the Western Union crew were flabbergasted. Charlie's mouth, in particular, was parted wide enough to admit a swarm of flies.

Darr was gawking at the prone forms in disbelief, but Wood was beaming like a kid just given a hatful of hard candy. "Serves them right!" he exclaimed.

Honest Jack came around the end of the bar, his eyes as large as saucers. "They're getting blood all over my floor!" he complained, then scanned the room and cheered up considerably. "Nothing was busted, though. How about that! Miracles do happen."

Darr tore his gaze from the spreading scarlet pool. "Is everyone in this godforsaken land insane? Come on." He seized Wood by the arm and hauled him toward the door. "We're getting out of here."

Wood glanced at Fargo and silently mouthed, "Thank you."

The door slammed in their wake, rousing the other workmen. Melton fumbled in a pocket and slapped change on the counter. "We're leaving, too! I never should have stopped in the first place."

Within moments Fargo was alone with the buffalo hunter and the owner. Still covering Angus, Fargo polished off his drink, fished in his own pocket for some money, and paid Honest Jack. Then he backed out, snagging the Sharps along the way. "I'll leave this at the end of the corral. But don't get any ideas."

"Don't look at me," Stark said. "I'm not hankerin' to be turned into a sieve if I can help it."

Honest Jack was checking the pulses of the fallen. "The breed is dead, but Brody still has a heartbeat." He looked up. "What do you want me to do with him?"

"Bury him alive for all I care," Fargo answered. Pushing the door open with his shoulder, he peeked outside before committing himself. The covered wagon and the vans were lumbering into motion, the drivers cracking whips to goad their teams.

Darr and Wood were on the last van. Wood caught sight of Fargo in the doorway and gave a little wave.

"Hold that open for me, will you?" Honest Jack hollered as he commenced dragging the body of Pawnee Tom. To Angus Stark, he said, "I'll be back in just a minute to help doctor our friend."

"No hurry," the hunter said, as if Brody's life meant nothing to him.

Fargo propped the door with his foot until the owner had shambled past. Letting it close, he stepped toward the Ovaro, never taking his eyes off the burlap-covered window.

"Pssst! Hold on, hombre!" Honest Jack whispered. "There's something you should know." Dropping Pawnee Tom with a thud, he scurried over. "What you did wasn't too bright. You're new to these parts so maybe you haven't heard."

"Heard what?"

"About Tuck Garson and his pack of killers. Folks say Garson's favorite pastime is to stake out people he doesn't like and skin them alive."

Tales of Garson's brutal exploits had been spreading like wildfire across the frontier. It was claimed the man was more animal than human. "So what does that have to do with me?" Fargo asked.

"Well, I can't prove it, mind you, but I've suspected for sometime that Angus, Brody and Pawnee Tom were part of Tuck Garson's outfit." Honest Jack paused to let the full import sink in. "I hope to heaven I'm wrong, mister. Because if I'm not, the most vicious bunch of curly wolves this side of creation are going to be after your hide."